FALLING IN LOVE FOR THE FIRST TIME

THE MURPHY CLAN—FALLING IN LOVE SERIES
BOOK THREE

KATHY COATNEY

Windtree
Press

To all the pet owners who've loved and lost a pet. With love to Bandit, Gracie, Kiwi, Annabel, Tess, Nemo, and Sherlock.

ACKNOWLEDGMENTS

I've had a number of life-altering moments in my life, each special in their own way. The road to becoming a novelist has been smooth and rocky, but it has been an incredible journey because of those who have accompanied me.

My faithful email check-in pal, Jennifer Skullestad; my critique partners, Luann Erickson and Lisa Sorensen; my beta readers, Rebecca Clark and Jody Burchinal Sherin—you are my GPS to finding the end. Friends and family made the journey memorable—Susan Crosby, Karol Black, Diana McCollum, Tammy Lambeth, Karen Duvall, Marie Hart, Alison Wells, Paty Jager, and my family—Nick, Wade, Devin, and Collin, Jake and Emily and sweet Allie and Russell. I'm blessed to have had you all beside me.

I've also had the pleasure to work with several talented businesswomen: Laura Shin, my editor, Yvonne Betancourt, my formatter, TINB Ink, and Tara, my cover designer.

ALSO BY KATHY COATNEY

Thank you for reading *Falling in Love for the First Time,* part of *The Murphy Clan.* *The Murphy Clan* can all be read as stand alone books, but there are also three series within the Clan—*Falling in Love, Return to Hope's Crossing, Crooked Halo Christmas Chronicles,* and a *Vermont Christmas Romance.* If you enjoyed the characters of Paradise Falls, be sure and check out the Falling in Love series and the entire Murphy Clan.

If you liked this book, I'd love it if you'd leave a review at Goodreads and BookBub.

I love hearing from my fans. You can contact me through my website, newsletter, or join my Facebook group Kathy Coatney's The Beauty Bowl. I share information about my books, excerpts, and other fun information. If you like free books come join Kathy Coatney's Review Team by sending me an email kathy@kathycoatney.com.

All my books are small town, contemporary romances with uplifting stories of hope, a sprinkling of quirky characters and a happily ever after.

Contact me at:

Website

Kathy Coatney's The Beauty Bowl

The Murphy Clan

Falling in Love series

Falling For You...Again

Falling in Love With You

Falling in Love For The First Time

Falling in Love With Him

Return to Hope's Crossing series

Forever His

Forever Mine

Forever Yours

Crooked Halo Christmas Chronicles

Be My Santa Tonight

Her Christmas Wish

Under the Mistletoe

A Vermont Christmas Romance

Santa Comes to Snowside

Box Set

Falling in Love Box Set

Crooked Halo Christmas Chronicles Box Set

Falling in Love for the First Time: From rivals to lovers.

She has a career she loves and a man she'd die for—her life is complete until tragedy strikes without waning.

Flight nurse Maggie Gregorio knows her husband has demons, but she's never seen what happens when they're unleashed. Never experienced the terror. The helplessness. Until she watches the man she loves more than life itself become a stranger.

Symptom free for years, Daniel is married to his soulmate, running his own emergency medical service, and he's able to provide safe refuge to his brother returning from deployment. Life is perfect...

Until the first unprovoked flash of anger. PTSD—Daniel's invisible enemy—resurfaces. A stranger even to himself, he transforms their home into an emotional warzone. And he has no idea how to stop this stranger he's become.

Now their very lives hang in the balance. Is their love strong enough to overcome the darkness that lies between them?

Get your copy today because true love only comes once in a lifetime!

CONTENTS

1

Paradise Falls, Idaho

T he sun flashed through the thick cluster of pine, cedar, and maple trees as Maggie Gregorio finished her last lap around Trinity Lake.

Maggie stopped at the edge of the lake and unclipped Lightning's leash so the four-year old white Lab could cool his feet and slurp water.

She shaded her eyes against the shimmering light reflecting off the glassy water—calm and serene—the exact opposite of the emotions roiling inside of her.

While Lightning drank, the faint sounds of a loudspeaker drifted across the water.

"The second annual Colin Gregorio triathlon begins in an hour."

Maggie snapped on Lightning's leash, paused a moment to absorb the quiet serenity, then walked around the lake to the triathlon and stepped in line for a cup of coffee.

Colin, her childhood friend and brother-in-law was gone, and all that was left of him was a triathlon in his memory.

Lightning pressed closer to her. Maggie stroked his head, taking comfort in his presence. She raised her face to the sun, picturing her adventure-junkie brother-in-law following the sunlight inching over the Canadian Rockies. The vision lightened her mood, and she hoped death had brought Colin peace and absolved him of the guilt he'd taken to the grave.

The line moved forward, and Maggie poured herself a cup of coffee, then stepped aside and fed Lightning a biscuit. He devoured it in a single bite.

A long line of contestants stood on the bank of Lake Trinity, the first leg of the triathlon. A one-mile swim in forty-five-degree water—damn cold even in a wetsuit, but doable.

"It's hard to believe it's November with as warm as it's been?"

Her ex-husband's voice melted over her like butter drizzled over hot pancakes. "I was thinking the same thing. Last year we had a foot of snow on the ground by now," she said.

Maggie's eyes met Daniel's, and her pulse kicked up as if she'd just run a marathon. It had been six months since their divorce. Why couldn't she move on? Because she still loved him, but she'd learned love alone couldn't keep a marriage together if there wasn't trust and communication. If only she'd told Daniel what had happened with Colin in Afghanistan. Instead he'd found Colin's journal and read it for himself. Maybe they could have salvaged their marriage instead of divorcing, but she'd promised Colin she'd keep his secret, and she had, but that had come at a price.

To make their break-up even stickier, she and Daniel were partners at Adventure Docs—emergency medical services combined with adventure sports. Colin's brainchild. He'd convinced Daniel to go into partnership with him and start the business while he finished his final tour in Afghanistan.

She eyed Daniel over the edge of her cup as he squatted down to pet Lightning. Maggie restrained herself from begging for some of that affection, but unlike her canine companion, Daniel no longer showered her with his love and attention.

Daniel straightened and sipped his water. "Even with as warm as it's been it's entirely possible we'll see snow, maybe ice at the higher elevations. MD and I have our ear pieces in if you and Sloan need help."

Sloan, another member of Adventure Docs, was working the event with her, while Daniel and MD, the fourth member of the team, participated in the triathlon.

Daniel never balked when she took charge. That said a lot considering how close he and Colin had been—brothers, partners, best friends. He trusted her to handle the event and never second-guessed her decisions.

"Thanks. I'm hoping nothing happens so we don't have to pull you out of the race." Maggie intended to make sure the event went off without a hitch.

MD joined them as Daniel's shoulders stiffened. "What the hell is he doing here?"

Maggie glanced at the sign-in table where Dr. Rutherford stood in line,. She'd had numerous altercations with him when she'd worked as a flight nurse for Paradise General. She'd loved the job, but not Rutherford's arrogance. She'd resigned after Colin left his half of Adventure Docs to her.

MD slugged down some water, then swiped the back of his wrist across his mouth. "I would guess he's racing."

A scowl pinched Daniel's features as he focused on MD, his old military buddy, a burly brute of a man. "Still can't keep from stating the obvious."

"Still can't keep from asking stupid questions."

Maggie pressed her lips together to restrain a smile and changed the subject. "So, are you ready to jump into that water?"

A gleam of excitement lit MD's eyes that reminded her of Colin. "Abso-damn-lutely." He waved a hand at the crystal blue sky. "A beautiful day for a brutal workout."

The man thrived on competition as did all the Adventure Docs, Maggie included.

MD nodded at her thigh. "How's the hammy?"

"Are you injured?" Daniel asked.

Maggie waved off his question. "Just a strained hamstring I've been babying. I did a ten-mile run on Elk Ridge yesterday and didn't have any problem."

MD held up his hand. "Hooah. That's one nasty trail. Give me five."

Maggie smacked his palm, pride filling the empty space left after her breakup with Daniel. She'd rather have Daniel, but since she couldn't have him, she poured herself into workouts so intense she couldn't think about how much she missed him.

MD nodded toward Dr. Rutherford. "So that's the prick you worked with."

Maggie nodded. "In all his glory."

MD studied him. "Christ, how old is he?"

"Seventy."

He whistled. "No offense, Mags, but I give the guy credit for being able to participate at his age."

Maggie agreed. Her only beef with the man was that he bullied everyone he worked with, but especially women.

Daniel's voice flowed over her, and her damn, stupid heart pumped double time. "I'm glad you're not working with him any more."

Maggie ignored her physical reaction and focused on Daniel's support. She nodded. "Me, too."

Christopher *Pretty Boy* Sloane, slung an arm over her shoulder. "Did I miss out on any hot gossip?"

Sloane might be nicknamed Pretty Boy, but the guy never hesitated to get his hands dirty, whether it was dealing with an emergency or tracking through mud and muck to reach a mountain top.

Maggie grinned. "Nothing worth repeating."

"Well, damn. I was hoping for something juicy."

Maggie shrugged. "Sorry."

Another announcement about the race.

"Come on, Pretty Boy. We've got work to do."

Sloane gave her a mock salute. "Yes, Boss. Lead the way."

From anyone else she might have taken it as a slur, but not from Sloane or anyone at Adventure Docs. They all treated her with respect as a skilled colleague who was damn good at her job, as well as an accomplished athlete, just like the rest of them.

Maggie hoisted her medical bag onto her shoulder and Lightning rose. "Good luck, boys."

The intensity of Daniel's stare burned into her back. She checked the urge to run back and throw herself into his arms. But she couldn't do that because Daniel didn't want her anymore.

~

MD's VOICE drew Daniel's attention away from where Maggie and Sloane had disappeared into the crowd.

"You know you could have her if you wanted her."

His personal life was off limits, especially today. He needed to focus on getting through the event and making Colin proud by punishing his body and forgetting all the ways he'd screwed up the relationships in his life.

Liam Murphy, Maggie's brother, joined them. "Hey, who's ready to get their asses kicked?"

Grateful for his old friend's arrival, Daniel slapped a hand on his shoulder. "Thought you might have chickened out."

Liam scowled at him and MD hooted out a laugh. "Wishful thinking."

Daniel narrowed his eyes at his colleague, friend, and old military buddy. "Is that a fact?"

"Damn straight it is. You're getting soft." MD punched him in the belly.

Daniel swallowed a groan. "Care to place a wager on that?"

MD reached into his back pocket, then held up both hands. "Left my wallet in the car, but I'll bet twenty."

Liam adjusted the straps on his swim goggles. "I'd get the money up front."

MD scowled at him. "I take offense to that."

"How can you take offense to the truth?" Liam asked, the amusement in his voice fading away as they headed over to the starting line. "Isn't that Dr. Rutherford?"

Daniel nodded.

Liam turned to MD. "Twenty says I'll beat that bastard."

MD looked from Liam to Rutherford. "By how much? I mean the guy's got thirty-five years on you."

"By an hour."

MD stroked his chin as he thought over the bet, then held out his hand. "Deal. If I lose I owe you twenty, but if I win, I get beer and dinner at Brother Murphy's—all I can eat and drink."

"Christ, that'll bankrupt me."

MD winked at him. "Then you'd better not lose."

Daniel didn't need to bet to show up Rutherford. He'd leave the guy in the dust, but what he wanted was to hear him apologize to Maggie for the way he'd treated her.

His gaze darted to Maggie and Sloan standing next to the Adventure Doc van. Maggie's eyes met his and Daniel's gut tightened. If only he could roll the clock back and change the past.

~

MAGGIE'S GAZE locked with Daniel's, and she longed for a do-over, a chance to go back and undo the pain they'd inflicted on each other.

She shook off the notion. Regret had been the kryptonite of their relationship. All she could do now was learn from her mistakes and move on.

"Maggie."

She turned and saw her sister-in-law, Abby, walking toward her with her two-year-old nephew, Jon. Maggie hugged her, then scooped Jon into her arms. He gave her a slobbery kiss that felt like heaven.

She ruffled his hair and settled him on her hip. "What are you doing here?"

Jon pointed to the runners with a pudgy finger. "Da."

Maggie's eyes went wide. "Noah's in the race?"

Jon reached for his mother, and Maggie handed him back. "Liam taunted him into signing up. I don't know what he was thinking."

Maggie spotted Noah standing beside Daniel and made a sweeping study of her brother. "He's still in decent shape."

Abby bumped her shoulder. "He's in excellent shape. What I meant was, I don't know why he lets you guys prod him into doing these things."

Maggie grinned. "It's the Murphy way."

"And something I will never understand."

"Da!"

Noah turned and grinned at his son, then gave him a thumbs-up.

Jon held out his arms and called to him again, clearly wanting to join his father.

"And here's another up and coming Murphy with the competitive gene."

Abby rolled her eyes. "God help me."

Jon cried for his father again and Abby cuddled him close. "He'll be back soon. We're going to watch him swim."

Sloan squatted in front of Jon. "Hey, pal, want to help Uncle Sloan check the medical gear in the van?"

Jon's tears dissolved, and a bright smile lit up his face, followed by a single swift nod.

"Come on then." Sloan climbed into the van.

Abby set him down and he raced forward, then halted when she didn't move. "Mama, come."

She took his hand and followed with Maggie and Lightning bringing up the rear.

"He's a typical male Murphy," she whispered to Abby.

"How so?"

"He's got all the women in his life wrapped around his finger."

Abby ruffled his fluffy blond hair. "And that's a bad thing?"

"No, it just shows me he's got a mother who loves him dearly."

Tears glistened in Abby's eyes. "That he does." She paused a moment then said in a choked whisper, "For the longest time I thought I'd never have a family of my own, and now it's like a gift from Jon."

Abby, Noah, and Jon, her first husband, had been best friends growing up. After Jon had died of ALS, Noah and Abby married. A sad story with a happy ending.

Abby lifted Jon into the trailer, and she was about to follow when her face paled. She leaned around the side of the van and promptly threw up.

"Mama," Jon wailed.

Sloan quickly drew the little boy's attention to the evac splint inside the trailer. He laid down on it and told Jon to strap him in. Jon looked out the door, and then at the splint. The splint won.

Maggie pulled back Abby's hair and rubbed her back until she finished vomiting. "You okay?"

Abby sat back on her haunches and inhaled a couple of deep breaths. "Do you have any water?"

Maggie reached inside the trailer, grabbed a bottle, and handed it to her.

Abby rinsed her mouth, spit, then took a long drink. "Thanks."

"Can I assume I'm going to be an aunt again?"

Abby's face glowed under the pallor. "Yes."

"And my brother is over the moon I suppose."

"He is and ready to shout it from the rooftops."

Maggie studied the painful expression on Abby's face. "But you're not."

Abby shrugged and leaned back against the fender. "I just wanted to wait to tell everyone until we were certain this time." She looked up at her, her eyes brimming with tears. "We miscarried six months ago."

Maggie squatted down beside her and hugged her. "I'm so sorry. Why didn't you tell me?"

Abby's voice wobbled. "It's not easy to talk about."

Why was it easier to be silent about emotional pain? At least Abby had had Noah and her gram to lean on.

Abby squeezed her hand. "I'm sorry I didn't tell you."

"It's okay. Just know I'm here for you if you ever need to talk."

"I know and thanks."

"Mama, look." Jon's squeal echoed from inside.

Abby rose, her color much improved from a few minutes ago. "I will be glad to be past this stage."

Maggie smiled, but acknowledged she'd be willing to puke the full nine months if she could have Daniel's baby.

Not gonna happen.

Damn know-it-all voice. She knew it wasn't going to happen, but it still didn't mean she couldn't hold onto that dream for just a little longer.

∿

THE GUN WENT OFF and Daniel dove into the water. He pushed himself hard, his own private demons nipping at his heels. He did his best to outswim them, but it seemed that no matter how hard he pushed, they were always there—like the ghost of Christmas past, except this was the ghost of failure that haunted his days and nights.

The friends he'd lost in Afghanistan—check.

The men he hadn't been able to save when a mission went bad —check.

The brother he adored—check.

The woman he loved beyond reason—check.

Maybe the first three had been out of his control, but walking away from Maggie had been a conscious decision.

He reached the shore, leaving the crystal clear water, his feet sinking into the muddy shoreline.

Daniel ripped off his goggles as MD came up alongside him, shaking his head and sending a spray of water over him. "Hey, man. You're swimming like we've got a whole platoon on our tails."

Daniel cast a sidelong glance at him and mimicked Colin's favorite phrase. "Go big or go home."

"This is more like go gargantuan or go home."

Daniel shrugged and kicked up his pace, heading for his bike. MD stayed with him.

Liam caught up a minute later. "Geez, where's the fire?"

"See," MD said, "I'm not the only one who thinks you're running like hellfire is on your ass."

Sunshine angled through a pair of white, fluffy clouds over the mountain range, the snowy peaks glistening in the muted light as Daniel eased his pace just slightly to slide into his shoes. He climbed on his bike and took off, passing the checkpoint with water, and Sloan, ready and waiting in case of a medical emergency. Maggie would be at the next checkpoint where they switched to running. She and Sloan leapfrogged the course so they were available at all the checkpoints. It kept them on the move, but he knew that's how they liked it. It was how the entire team liked it, and why they were all a part of Adventure Docs. They went where they were needed.

MD came abreast of him and gave Sloan the finger as they rode past. "Did you see Pretty Boy back there messing with his hair while we're out here busting our balls?"

Sloan was anything but a pretty boy. He'd been stuck with the name when they were in the military because the women flocked to him. More than a few in their unit had been envious of his ability to attract women with such ease.

In truth, the women hadn't flocked to him because of his good looks, but because he had a way of making them feel special and appreciated.

Maybe he should have taken pointers from Sloan. Then he and Maggie would still be married. No, they wouldn't because he still would have left her.

~

MAGGIE LUGGED her medical bag to the side-by-side ATV. Lightning leapt into the back as she took the rough, rutted service road to the next checkpoint.

The dense forest blotted out the sunlight. Wide, sweeping

branches brushed the sides of the ATV, releasing the fresh, clean scent of pine that always brought an image of Daniel to mind.

She reached the next checkpoint where participants switched from bikes to running. This section narrowed and turned rocky, but it didn't stop participants from hurtling down the mountain to the finish line.

She'd just stowed her gear when a rider rode up, shouting, "Help! Help! A guy crashed over here."

Maggie grabbed her medical bag, Lightning at her side, and ran to the embankment where the rider had fallen onto a ledge about six feet below.

Maggie hoisted the bag over her shoulder, told Lightning to stay, and carefully made her way down, the crushed cinder sliding out from under her feet. She skidded several times, but finally made it to the ledge and her patient.

She kneeled beside him and swore when she recognized him— Dr. Raymond B. Rutherford.

Maggie spoke into her com. "Sloan, I've got a participant down just before the last checkpoint. Bring the evac splint."

"On my way."

Daniel's voice came over the com. "MD and I are on the way, too."

"Finish the race first."

"Already did."

Of course they had. Maggie took out her stethoscope, and Dr. Rutherford opened his eyes. He stared up at her, his face twisted with pain.

"Don't want you...touching me," he wheezed out.

Maggie didn't want to treat him, either, and she wished like hell Sloan had been on this leg of the race.

"Sorry, I'm afraid you're stuck with me until the rest of the team arrives. I promise you, you're in good hands, *Doctor*." *He* might not be professional, but Maggie would be. "Take a deep breath."

He glared at her, then finally inhaled a short breath. "Leave me alone," he said, his voice barely a whisper of sound.

He might not like her, but instinct told her his reaction had more to do with the pain he was in.

She spoke quietly into the com. "Got a possible pneumothorax."

Daniel's voice came back calm and professional. "Copy that."

Sloan arrived with the evac splint.

"I don't want her. Get me someone else," he told Sloan.

Sloan merely grinned in response. Nothing ruffled him. "Maggie's the best, Dr. Rutherford."

Dr. Rutherford's dismissive gaze told that her no nurse would ever be good enough. Daniel and MD arrived. With the whole team here, they didn't need her. She quickly gathered her gear and exchanged places with Sloan, then climbed up the embankment.

Daniel grabbed her hand and helped her over the top. His touch sent a tingle of awareness up her arm. He must have felt it, too, because he immediately released her.

Maggie quickly stepped back, hoisted her bag over her shoulder, then called Lightning, and headed back to the van without a word to Daniel. They were over, and she had the divorce papers to prove it, but whenever he touched her, her heart insisted otherwise.

~

MAGGIE STARED out the living room window at Lake Serenity the next morning. Dark clouds hovered overhead, heavy and ready to dump more rain. The wind ruffled the water, whipping it into a gray, brooding froth that mimicked the emotions churning through her on the two-year anniversary of Colin's death.

She spun away from the window. She had to get out of the house and the break in the weather offered her an opportunity to get outside and hike to Devil's Peak—Colin's favorite spot. She couldn't think of a better way to remember the Space Cowboy—the nickname she'd given Colin from his favorite song. There was no question he'd been a grinner and a sinner. He'd also been the one to hurl headlong into danger, dragging Maggie with him. She'd never been able to resist a challenge, but she'd never taken the foolish chances Colin had, which became even riskier after he'd left the military. It wasn't until after he died that she fully understood why.

She grabbed a quick breakfast, then loaded her SUV. She called Lightning and he leapt into the back. She closed the rear hatch and reached the trailhead twenty minutes later, surprised to find it loaded with cars, forcing her to park at the far end. She'd expected most would avoid the trails after the torrential rains had left them slick and muddy. She would have, too, if not for the driving need to be close to Colin.

She grabbed her pack and hiking poles, then she and Lightning set off. The trail took a sharp, steep turn almost immediately. Most hikers took the other trail because it required a lower level of proficiency.

Maggie smiled when Colin's voice came to her.

Now, how can you beat a trail that gets your heart pumping from the get-go?

She couldn't argue with his logic, and it was the reason she loved it, too.

Maggie focused on her breathing as the crisp November air nipped at her nose and cheeks. An eagle soared above her, and her gaze tracked it to its nest high in a burned-out pine tree. A squirrel scurried across the path, then stopped and chattered as if chastising her for invading his territory.

The brush rustled and a moment later a doe leapt into the path. Maggie stumbled to a halt, grabbing Lightning's collar. The doe froze, her wide, dark eyes fixed on Maggie a long moment before it bounded into the forest.

Maggie relaxed and released Lightning, murmuring "good boy" before resuming their hike. She normally made the top in a little over two hours, but today she pushed it, needing to burn off her pent-up emotions. Thirty minutes into the hike she stopped to rest. She lifted her face toward the sky, inhaling a deep breath of damp air. A light, misty rain fell over her as she started hiking again. She and Lightning reached the top at one hour, forty-five minutes—a personal best.

She climbed up onto Colin's boulder, braced her feet, and

pumped both fists into the air, reaching out to Colin and feeling closer to him than she had in a long, long time.

Muted sunlight cut through the cluster of clouds and shone down on

her. The breeze carried Colin's voice.

I'm here. I'm okay. Don't worry about me.

"I miss you," she whispered back, the lump in her throat threatening to cut off her air supply.

She swallowed. *No more sorrow.*

She pushed aside her grief, determined to enjoy the rest of the hike. She grabbed a dog biscuit from her backpack and fed it to Lightning, then leaned back against the boulder and munched on a nutrition bar while she watched a pair of eagles soar overhead.

A rumble of thunder echoed as she finished the bar. Stuffing the wrapper in her pack, she said, "Time to head back, boy."

Lightning rose, his tail wagging, as fresh and ready to go as if they'd just started.

Maggie shook her head in awe. Nothing wore him down.

They started back, taking the faster trail to beat the rain.

Raindrops splashed her face and rapidly increased in velocity. She pulled the plastic poncho from backpack and jammed it over her coat.

Within minutes the wind turned to a hurricane-force gale. Thunder rumbled. Maggie looked to the west. The dark clouds burst open. Water gushed from the sky like a burst dam, washing the trail out from under her feet.

Lightning struck the ground.

Maggie stumbled and nearly fell.

Another bolt shot out of the sky, striking the tree in front of her and severing it in half.

Maggie lost her footing and landed hard on the ground. Lightning pressed his nose to her cheek and whined. She wrapped an arm around him and hugged him close as her heart raced. Shaky and numb, she pushed to her feet and headed back in the opposite direction, searching for somewhere to take shelter.

The trail made a sharp left, but before she reached it, the ground trembled beneath her feet. She jumped back when a dozen elk stormed toward her, then veered away.

Her knees trembled and her pulse hammered. Lightning barked and jumped in front of her as a giant wall of water rushed toward them and a flash flood swept them over the side of the mountain.

2

Daniel stared out the tiny living room window of his apartment, the only view was of the parking lot and one rattletrap, grimy mini-van owned by his neighbor. A lot like his life—sad and lonely. He abruptly turned away and went to dress.

He spent more and more of his time at the office rather than his silent, empty apartment. The quiet drove him crazy. No Maggie. No Colin. Nothing.

And today of all days the void made him painfully aware of all that was missing in his life. It had been two years since Colin had died, but it felt like yesterday. His brother had put laughter in his life, joy in his heart, but as much as he'd loved him, he'd resented Colin's relationship with Maggie. The way they'd communicated with just a look and a nod. Daniel had wanted that with her.

He finished dressing and poured a cup of coffee, then searched the tiny kitchen for sugar.

Nothing.

He knew without looking he had no cream. In fact, the state of his refrigerator mimicked his life—an empty cavern. He never ate here, just slept when he had no other choice, and many nights he crashed at the office rather than confront what his life had become.

He sipped the coffee and grimaced. Bracing himself, he took another drink, then shuddered and dumped it down the drain along with the rest in the pot. He grabbed his coat, raced through the downpour to his truck and drove over to his father's for breakfast, determined to be positive and upbeat.

As much as he hated to admit it, his dad was coping better than he was. He'd found a way to move forward while Daniel remained mired in the past.

He rang the bell and soft, feminine footsteps echoed out to him. The door swung open and Amanda Wilcox, his father's girlfriend, wrapped him in her arms. "I'm so glad you came."

She smelled of fresh baked bread and cinnamon, just as she had when she'd been his kindergarten teacher. He wanted nothing more than to remain in her arms and absorb every bit of her warmth and strength, but he pulled back.

"Thanks for inviting me, M—Amanda," he amended before she reminded him to call her by her given name. She would forever be Mrs. Wilcox to him.

Amanda had been his surrogate mother, too, after his mom had died in the car accident.

Her blue eyes warmed with love. "Daniel, this is your home. You don't need to tiptoe around here. Treat it like you did before your dad and I started dating."

He tried, he really did, but he still felt like the interloper. "I'm working on it."

She shook her head and made a *tsking* sound as he followed her to the kitchen where his father was putting the finishing touches on breakfast. He went straight to the coffee pot and poured a cup, adding a generous amount of cream.

"I just made that coffee. It's hotter than hell."

Daniel ignored the warning and scalded the inside of mouth. He didn't care. The need for caffeine overrode common sense.

"You always were the more stubborn one." His dad grinned, but it didn't reach his eyes.

True. Colin had been the golden boy, always easygoing and agreeable.

Amanda filled the painful silence by ushering them to the table. "Let's eat before the food gets cold."

Breakfast smelled heavenly, but Daniel wasn't hungry, especially when the empty chair beside him was a stark reminder of the emptiness inside of him. He wanted Colin seated next to him, legs extended and crossed at the ankles, and wearing that cocky grin as he retold his most recent adventure.

His father launched into his standard do-you-remember-when stories of Colin—his way of keeping his son alive in his mind and heart. Daniel would never deny him his coping technique even if the trip down memory lane left him raw and hollowed out like a Halloween pumpkin.

"Even when you were kids he would always climb the tallest tree. Remember the time he climbed the stadium lights on the football field at Paradise High and fell asleep? He scared the bejesus out of me. When he came down I'd intended to ground him for the rest of his life, but the absolute serenity on his face stopped me. I knew then and there that if I punished him for something that gave him that kind of tranquility, I'd destroy the part of him that made him who he was."

He'd made the right call, but there was a part of Daniel that wished his father had locked Colin in his room until the adventure junkie was exorcised from him. Even thinking it, he knew it wouldn't have made a difference because doing so would have destroyed the Colin he'd loved.

Amanda launched into a do-you-remember-when story that he'd heard a dozen times. That was the problem with the dead. There were never new stories, just regurgitated ones.

The first year they'd had breakfast on Colin's angel day as Amanda called it, Maggie had still been at his side, but the strain between them had been obvious and uncomfortable. Still, he'd take discomfort over divorce.

He pushed his food around his plate, his appetite MIA.

His dad squeezed his forearm. "Are the eggs too runny?"

Daniel stared at the weather-beaten hand, reminding him time marched on, that someday he would lose his dad just as he'd lost Colin. And then he would be truly and completely without family. Maggie had been the buffer to that reality.

He raised his eyes and forced a smile. "No, they're fine."

He hadn't fooled anyone with the lie. They knew as well as he did the loss of his appetite loss was emotional. He managed to choke down the rest of his toast to satisfy Amanda and sipped coffee the rest of the meal.

Afterward he helped clean up, and the subject moved to the race the day before.

"I hear Dr. Rutherford took a nasty spill." There was a bit of evil delight in his father's expression that Daniel couldn't help but share.

"He did. He's going to be laid up for a while."

"Couldn't have happened to a nicer guy."

His father's mild tone belied his real feelings. They felt the same way about the man, but even so, Daniel didn't wish the man ill will.

"Your girl didn't deserve to be treated like that."

Maggie wasn't his girl anymore and never would be again, no matter how much he wished otherwise and it was a good thing. He had demons besides Colin he was fighting, and he didn't want her in the middle of them. He finished wiping the counter, then hugged his father and whispered in his ear, "She didn't, Dad."

They held each other a long moment, then Daniel pulled back. "I've got to get to work. I'm glad you and Amanda are spending the day together."

His dad looped an arm around Amanda's waist and pulled her close. Daniel experienced a wave of envy. He wanted what his father and Amanda had—he wanted Maggie.

Daniel pressed a kiss to Amanda's cheek. "Thanks for breakfast."

Her eyes glistened. "Anytime."

He knew she meant it, and he would be back and stay longer, just not today. He climbed into his truck, and the pressure in his chest began to ease.

He stared sightlessly out the windshield, wishing yet again that Colin had never followed him into the military, that he'd never seen the things he'd seen. Maybe then the nightmares and the sudden flares of anger would stop.

Colin's stint in the military had made him the ultimate risk taker, all because of an incident on his final tour in Afghanistan. He might not have died in action, but his death was a direct result of his military career.

~

WHEN DANIEL ARRIVED at the office, Sloan was already there sipping coffee. Daniel poured himself a cup, grunted a greeting at Sloan, then stepped out on the deck and watched as more clouds built over the horizon. Just hours after the race, it had started raining with barely a break in the downpour for the past eighteen hours. The rivers and streams were swollen and overflowing with water. To make matters worse, the temperatures were predicted to drop drastically and turn to snow this afternoon.

While the clouds didn't look particularly threatening, that could change on a dime. Fall equaled unpredictable weather in this part of the country.

Sloan came out and leaned against the railing. "I wasn't sure you'd be in today."

Daniel cast a sideways glance at him. "It's a workday. Why wouldn't I be here?"

Sloan's lazy grin matched the amusement in his eyes. "With the way you pushed it yesterday I figured you'd be laid up in bed."

Daniel lifted his right leg, the muscles protesting the movement, and schooled a blank expression. "I'm fine. How are you doing?"

Sloan scowled at him. "I hate showoffs." He sipped his coffee, then shot him a sly grin. "So if you're in such fine form today, what do you say we do a workout before MD arrives?"

A workout was the last thing Daniel wanted, but he'd never admit it. "Sure, why not." He gulped down the last of his coffee, and they went to the basement that held a state-of-the-art gym.

He lifted a moderately heavy barbell and sucked back a groan. Every movement was a painful reminder of the rigors he'd put his body through the day before, but a workout beat the hell out of focusing on Colin and Maggie.

He peered closely at Sloan and wasn't so sure the man hadn't devised the challenge to take his mind off the memories flooding him. And what if he had? Shouldn't he be grateful he had a friend who cared enough to inflict physical rather than mental pain?

～

Sweat drenched Daniel's body, and he had new aches and pains after they finished, but he felt better. He showered again and went upstairs to find MD at his desk.

MD swiveled his chair around and scanned him from head to toe. "Looks like Sloan didn't kill you."

Daniel snorted. "Not from lack of trying."

MD grunted and took a swig of his coffee.

"How long have you been up here?"

"Long enough to hear the weights clanking and you two swearing. Sloan getting all dolled up?"

"Yeah."

A mock scowl came over MD's face. "That oughta take all morning."

"I heard that," Sloan called up from the basement.

MD shook his head. "I swear he's got supersonic hearing."

Daniel hid a smile and poured himself a glass of water. Those two had perfected the art of squabbling. Maggie claimed she'd seen their names listed in the dictionary under bickering.

"Where's Maggie?"

"She said she'd be late." MD took a sheet of paper from his desk without missing a beat and read off their schedule for the day, which included putting together two training sessions—one for the Air Force and one for a search-and-rescue group.

They went through the drill they'd prepared for the Air Force, working out some of the rough edges, then took a break. All three of them were drenched in sweat and breathing heavily by the time they finished.

"Good thing Maggie's not here because she would have pushed us to keep going and probably killed us before it was over." MD shook his head. "And you two idiots worked out before. What were you thinking?"

Daniel managed a smile. "He challenged me. What could I do?"

"Be the smarter man," MD shot back.

They both knew he wouldn't have walked away from the challenge, either. Not a single member of Adventure Docs, including Maggie and especially Colin, ever turned down a challenge. It wasn't in their DNA.

Sloan wheezed in a breath of air. "You talk big, but if I challenged you right now, you'd drag your sorry ass up and accept."

MD grunted in response. "Let's hope Maggie's out on a long run so we don't have to keep up with her when she gets here."

A silent agreement went through the three of them. Maggie might be small, but she had the endurance of an Energizer Bunny, and she put them all to shame.

Daniel checked the time.

Eleven. She should have been here by now.

Sloan pushed to his feet, uttering a groan. "She's probably gone a little farther than usual—at least that's what I'm praying is keeping her for all our sakes." He grabbed a sports drink, twisted off the cap, and took a long swallow.

The phone rang and Sloan went inside to answer it, returning a minute later. "That was the sheriff's department. A flash flood warning has just been issued. They're asking for our assistance."

Daniel glanced to the sky. Dark, threatening clouds loomed on the horizon. "Let's move." He headed inside to collect his gear. "Sloan, you man the phones here and call Maggie. We're going to need all hands on deck."

Sloan disappeared into the media room and started making calls while Daniel and MD loaded the van. They put in their ear coms and Sloan's voice came through. "Sheriff's department just called with an update. They had a flash flood at Pine Ridge."

"Copy that. We're leaving now. Did you reach Maggie?"

"No, it went straight to voice mail."

Maggie always answered her phone. "Keep trying her cell, and her house, and keep me posted."

"You got it," Sloan said.

Once upon a time he'd have known exactly where Maggie was, but no more. He'd let her slip through his fingers, and he'd lost her as surely as he'd lost Colin.

3

Ten years ago...

Maggie's last class ended and she sprinted out the door. Freedom! Two o'clock and still plenty of time to make it back to the apartment and get a run in. The apartment she shared with Colin sat on the outskirts of Wilson Creek not far from the college in central Idaho.

She entered the apartment minutes later, changed into her running clothes, and hit the trail. She should be studying, but fresh air and the hills beckoned. She needed the wind in her face and the sun on her back or she'd go stark, raving mad.

She forgot about school, she forgot about studying, she forgot about everything except her conversation with Colin yesterday when he'd asked her when she was going to admit she had feelings for his brother.

She'd wanted to deny his question had merit, but how could she when all she ever thought about was Daniel?

Not that it mattered since she didn't even know when she'd see him again.

Colin's smile had turned devious, and he'd taken pleasure in announcing that Daniel would be sleeping on their sofa for the next two weeks while he was on leave.

Rather than being overjoyed at the news, she'd felt sick to her stomach. Two weeks. How would she hide her feelings for that long?

Coward.

Ha! Tell him she cared about him when he only saw her as his best friend's little sister? Not likely.

Bawk, bawk, bawk.

Damned annoying voice. But...maybe it was time she put herself out there and actually do something besides pine for him.

What if she told him and he rejected her? What if he didn't? What if Colin was right and Daniel actually had feelings for her, but they held each other at arm's length for fear of rejection?

Stop it!

She'd come to run, not agonize over Daniel. She passed several other runners and smiled and nodded.

"Excuse me."

A runner came up behind her, and she moved over to let him pass, then nearly stumbled and fell when her gaze locked with Daniel's. He slowed his pace and ran alongside her.

"Well, fancy meeting you here."

This was no accident. Colin had to have told him she'd be here.

"Fancy that." She glanced at him, then back at the trail. "Of all the trails in the world, you end up on the same one as me."

His eyes twinkled with merriment. "What luck, huh?"

She said nothing in response as she couldn't form a coherent thought.

He continued to keep pace with her.

"Don't let me hold you back." The trail took a sharp incline and Maggie's breathing increased.

"You're not. If I want a workout, I can run anytime since I'm on leave."

Her temper inched up along with her breathing. Was he implying this wasn't a workout?

Making small talk became an effort, so she focused on the run, the distance she'd come and still had to go—anything but the Adonis beside her who sent her pulse rate soaring into triple digits.

You're a champion, Maggie girl.

Her father's words spurred her to pick up her pace. She might not have Daniel's stride, but she had heart and that counted for a hell of a lot.

When she reached the top, she glanced over at Daniel. He'd barely broken a sweat while her shirt clung to her. Damn him and his long, sinewy legs that had six inches on her.

"How about dinner after the run?"

"No time. Gotta meet my study group tonight." What was wrong with her? He'd invited her to dinner, the moment she'd been waiting for, and she'd immediately turned him down.

He gave her a long probing stare, then shrugged. "Okay, but if you change your mind it's an open invitation." He picked up his pace and disappeared around the corner literally leaving her in the dust.

It galled her how easily he disappeared up the trail and that her heart had gone along with him.

∼

MAGGIE SLIPPED OUT of the apartment early the next morning, tiptoeing past Daniel sprawled out on the sofa. Resisting the urge to trace her fingers over the chiseled muscles visible above the blankets, she grabbed her backpack and headed to her first class.

By mid-morning, she was starving. She reached into her back-pack for a nutrition bar as she crossed campus to her next class, then came to a halt when she rammed into none other than Daniel Gregorio. Not doubt Colin's matchmaking at work again.

"Oh, sorry." She started walking and he strolled alongside her.

Another attack of nerves struck, leaving her tongue-tied. "W-W-What are you doing here?"

"Walking."

Suspicion bloomed. This definitely had Colin's handiwork written all over it. Not a surprise, knowing Colin. He loved meddling in other people's affairs, but Daniel would never be swayed by his brother's interference, which meant he had to be here on his own volition. Did that mean he was interested in her?

"So your story is we just happened to meet up, the same way we just happened to be running the same trail yesterday?"

"Funny, huh?"

Not really. She wanted him to be here because he'd sought her out, not because Colin put him up to it.

"So how was the run, Forrest?"

Maggie stopped and stared into the most startling blue eyes she'd ever seen. They were bluer than the glacial water in Lake Serenity. They reminded her of home and all the times he and her brother, Liam, pestered her. But behind the teasing there had been a gentleness that had always drawn her to him, and he'd always encouraged her no matter what she tried to do. She got so caught up in those eyes that she forgot his question until he prompted her.

"How was the run, Forrest?"

"Why are you calling me Forrest?"

That damn grin lifted the corners of his mouth and sent twin dimples creasing his cheeks. "You know Forrest, as in Forrest Gump."

"Forrest Gump from the movie?"

Dimples creased his cheeks again, and she had to forcibly restrain herself from kissing each one.

"Yes, Tom Hanks and Sally Field, best picture in 1994."

She rarely went to the movies and didn't watch much television, either. At her blank look, he said, "You're telling me you've never seen the movie."

She shook her head and started walking again. He kept pace with her. "Okay, we are having movie night tonight."

"Thanks, but I have another run planned."

He touched her arm and her pulse hammered out of control.

His voice held a raspy edge. "After the run, Forrest?"

She lifted her gaze to his and all she wanted was dinner and a movie with him, and so much more. But what if he *only* wanted dinner and a movie?

The only way to know for sure would be to accept his invitation.

Stalling, she asked, "Will I find out why you keep calling me Forrest?"

He fingers trailed across her cheek, sending an involuntary shiver through her. "Definitely."

She couldn't refuse, especially when she wanted more than anything to be with him.

"Come on, Maggie. You've got to have some fun in your life. Take pity on me. I've got no friends here, and my brother's more interested in partying than spending time with me."

He was pretty darned adorable when he begged. "Okay. I should be back by seven-thirty."

"I'll have the movie and popcorn ready." He held out his hand. She stared at it a long moment wondering if she'd misread his invitation.

The instant her skin made contact with his, she knew friendship was off the table because she wanted a hell of a lot more than a handshake.

❧

MAGGIE HEADED BACK to the apartment, her stomach rumbling with an insistent reminder that she hadn't eaten since lunch, but it would have to wait. She had a date with the man of her dreams, and she was *not* sitting through a movie reeking like a basketball team at halftime.

You didn't use to care how you smelled around him.

That was before.

She stepped into the apartment and the scent of marinara had her reconsidering her plan. Her stomach growled with approval.

"How was the run?" Daniel called from the kitchen.

Her nose led the way. "Great."

"Hope you're hungry. I made spaghetti and meatballs, Caesar salad, and French bread with garlic butter."

"Sounds and smells wonderful, but I've got to shower before I eat."

He waved a slice of bread under her nose. "Are you sure?"

She wavered until the odor wafting off her body overrode the delicious scents coming from the kitchen. With regret she turned for the bathroom.

"Ten minutes and then dinner." She whipped back around, snatched the bread from his hand, and headed to the bathroom. "Make that fifteen minutes," she called back. She needed time to put on a little makeup, too.

~

THE TINY DINING room table that usually served as a dumping spot had been cleared and set for an intimate dinner for two when Maggie returned to the kitchen fifteen minutes later. Their evening looked more and more like a date, and the rush of emotion put a giddy-up in her step.

Daniel came out of the kitchen with a bowl of pasta in one hand and sauce in the other. His gaze swept over her and his eyes twinkled with amusement. "Hey, you clean up nice." He glanced at the clock on the wall. "And punctual."

Punctual was not a word she associated with someone interested in her.

Daniel set the dishes on the table and pulled out a chair for her. "Sit and start dishing up while I grab the bread."

She piled her plate with plenty of pasta and meatballs, sprinkled it liberally with Parmesan cheese, then took a bite and moaned, savoring the rich flavors.

"Good?" he asked.

"Mmhmm." She swallowed. "Fantastic. I didn't know you cooked."

"I didn't, but after I joined the military and got my own place, it was learn or starve."

"What? You couldn't charm that harem of yours into cooking for you?" Maggie teased, but deep down she resented every one of those women.

He held out the bread and she took two slices. "How do you know about the women I date?"

Maggie gave him an exaggerated eye roll. "Colin, how else?"

"My brother needs to show some discretion and keep his mouth shut." He twirled pasta around his fork.

"Good luck with that. He thrives on butting into other people's business."

Daniel smiled, and something akin to revenge flickered in his eyes. "He and I will be having a discussion about that."

A sudden attack of nerves stole her appetite when she realized Daniel was truly attracted to her.

"Full already?" he asked.

She swallowed back her anxiety. "For now, but give me twenty minutes, and I'll, I'll be in the kitchen again." And hopefully her stomach would stop churning.

He chuckled. "I've got you covered with popcorn, a bag of licorice, and dessert."

Was it her imagination or did his tone imply dessert wasn't necessarily food, or was that wishful thinking on her part?

She placed a shaky hand over her chest. "Dessert, licorice, and popcorn, be still my heart. What's on the menu for dessert?"

The blue of his eyes deepened as he pretended to zip his lips closed. "It's a surprise."

"I hate surprises. Tell me."

"Sorry. You'll have to make do with popcorn and licorice while we watch the movie. *Dessert* is for after."

His emphasis on dessert tightened the knot in her stomach, but even so she managed to finish her salad, then help him clear the table. She tried to peek at the dessert, but he shooed her out of the kitchen with the bag of red and black licorice and a glass of root beer —her favorite, and she was impressed he'd remembered.

She sat on the sofa, opened the bag, and selected a red vine, then munched on it while she waited for Daniel.

He joined her with a giant bowl of popcorn, the heavenly scent of freshly melted butter whetting her appetite. He grabbed the remote and turned on the television, then sat down beside her—close enough their thighs bumped together. Suddenly her entire focus centered on the butterflies taking flight in her tummy from just the touch of Daniel's body to hers.

He set the popcorn on his lap and offered her some.

She took a handful as the movie started. She reached for more and her knuckles brushed his. Her gaze shot up, and his eyes smoldered with an intensity she'd never seen before.

She turned back to the movie, trying to focus on it, but she had no idea what was going on. All she could think about was how much she wanted him, and she'd face rejection to have him.

Daniel looped his arm behind the sofa and casually dropped his hand over her shoulder.

Her breathing accelerated, and her pulse thrummed in her ears. She didn't care. All she wanted was his body naked and pressed against her.

His voice whispered in her ear. "Maggie."

She tilted her head and found his face so close she saw his pupils expand.

"What?" Was that her voice that sounded breathless and achy with need?

"I want to kiss you."

She gave an imperceptible nod and trailed her fingers over the rough stubble on his cheeks. He captured her fingers and pressed them to his lips, then leaned in and replaced his fingers with his lips. She tasted popcorn, soda, and *him*.

His hands slid down her back, brushing up and down, sending tingles over her body. She sucked in a breath of air, then pressed her breasts to his chest, but it wasn't enough. She wanted all of him.

She twined her fingers through his and laid his hand over her breast.

He froze.

She looked into his eyes and saw regret. Her heart shuttered to a stop.

"I like you Maggie—a lot, but—"

She leapt from the sofa and held out a hand. "No buts. Either you're interested, or you're not." She held her ground, refusing to back down.

He set the popcorn on the coffee table and rose, standing so close his breath warmed her face. "I want you, so much my gut is twisted in knots, but I can't promise anything permanent."

"Did I ask you to?"

"No, but—"

"Stop with the buts. Do you care about me?"

"Yes."

"Do you want me?"

"Yes."

"Are you adding me to your list of conquests?"

"Hell, no, but—"

She pressed a finger to his lips. "I told you, no buts. I know once you leave here you'll be gone for months. I know what we'll be starting will be long distance. I'm okay with that. Are you?"

"Yes."

His eyes darkened and a whole different kind of tension filled her —joy, eagerness, impatience.

She raised up on tiptoe, brushing her lips against his, then pulled back and crooked a finger at him as she walked backward to the bedroom. "Then we'd better make the most of the time we have."

～

DAWN PEEKED through the bedroom window when Maggie woke the next morning, her body sprawled across Daniel's.

She propped her head in her hand and watched him sleep, his face soft in the early morning light filtering through the window. She couldn't resist tracing a finger along his jawline.

He stirred, stretched, then slowly opened his eyes. "Did you want something?" His lazy drawl sent her heart rat-tat-tapping in her chest.

"You."

Daniel yawned. "Since when do you do anything but sleep at this time of day?"

Her finger traveled from his chin to his navel. "While that is my preference, I've been known to make an exception for a worthy cause."

"And I'm the worthy cause?" His blue eyes turned cobalt with a fire that Maggie only wanted extinguished with her.

She swallowed around the growing knot of desire wedged in her throat. "Definitely."

He yawned again and stretched his arms overhead, then rolled onto his side. "I think I'd rather sleep a little longer." The teasing glint in his eyes dared her to object.

Challenge accepted. Maggie tossed back the covers. "Fine, get some *beauty sleep*." Not that he needed it. "I'm going to shower."

Before she moved off the bed, he snagged her around the waist and rolled her underneath him. "Sleep is overrated. I've got something else in mind."

Her voiced purred like a satisfied kitten. "Like what?"

His fingers slid up her thigh. "You."

"What about breakfast?"

"It's going to be a little late."

Who needed food when she had a man like Daniel in her bed?

❧

MAGGIE FOUND HERSELF SALIVATING AGAIN, except this time over Daniel's cooking, instead of the man himself. Although just watching him move around the kitchen, Maggie thought about skipping breakfast and having him instead.

Her stomach rumbled.

"You are a bottomless pit, Forrest."

"I still don't know why you keep calling me Forrest."

"Not my fault. You were the one who wanted to skip the movie."

Maggie leaned against the sink and shook a finger at him. "Oh no, you're not blaming that on me. It was a mutual decision."

Daniel leaned over and kissed her. "It was, and the best decision I've made in a long, long time."

Daniel turned back to the stove, and slid a perfectly grilled omelet onto her plate. "Sit and eat before you pass out from hunger."

She sat down at the bar and started eating with gusto. "This is fabulous. Are you sure they didn't train you as a cook instead of a medic?"

The toast popped. He placed two slices on her plate and some bacon.

His laughter echoed the tiny kitchen. "Hardly. They would have drummed me out of the Corps if they'd tasted my cooking back then." He held up the coffee pot. "More?"

Maggie pushed her mug toward him and mumbled her thanks around a bite of bacon.

"So what exactly are you doing in the military?" She had a general idea, but she wanted more detail.

Daniel filled his plate and poured himself more coffee, then joined her. "Actually, I've been asked to join an elite rescue team."

"Seriously?"

He scooped up a bite, nodding as he chewed.

"That's awesome. Congrats. What will you be doing?"

"I'll be training in combat search-and-rescue, combat medicine, and extended care."

Maggie arched a brow impressed. "Not everyone gets in, do they?"

"No, it's really difficult to get into, physically demanding, and ninety percent of the candidates that are accepted end up washing out or not finishing the program."

"I can't imagine you won't make it." She made a sweep of his body that she knew a lot more intimately than she had a few hours ago.

"Is that a fact?"

"It is."

"First one stripped and in bed wins." Maggie shoved back her chair to race for the bedroom, but he caught the back of her shirt and reeled her back without leaving his chair.

"What if I told you I didn't want to race, that I wanted to take it so slow you'd beg me to let you finish?"

His words fanned the flames of desire raging out of control. "I'd say who am I to argue with a man willing to make me beg?"

~

THE FRONT DOOR squeaked and woke Maggie. She and Daniel had fallen asleep after their latest round of lovemaking. Slipping out of bed, she eased the bedroom door closed.

Colin sat at the kitchen table, blotting blood from his forehead with a towel.

"What happened to you?"

He grinned. His teeth stood out through the thick layer of dust covering his face. "I was mountain biking."

She glanced at the clock and it was a few minutes to nine. "Were you out there at dawn?"

"Hell, no. We started about seven. I might be a daredevil, but I don't bike in the dark."

Maggie arched a brow. "Might be?"

Her comment drew a chuckle and a wince. "Don't make me laugh. I think I bruised a rib."

She stepped closer to get a better look at him and concern replaced teasing. "What exactly did you do?"

That swagger she knew so well radiated from him. "Mike and I hit McKenzie Trail early. We'd just made it over the top of those big boulders when I swerved to miss a branch and hit an overhead rock. It knocked me off my bike and down a six-foot embankment."

"And all you did was bang up your ribs?"

He gestured to his left ankle propped on the chair with a bag of ice on it. "I sprained up my ankle, too."

"I don't suppose you went to the hospital and got checked out?"

His smile, so like Daniel's, flashed again, all charm and a touch of the devil. "Hell, no." He grimaced when he moved his ankle. "I thought the worst part was having to walk my bike out two miles. Now I'm not so sure."

Maggie went to the kitchen and filled a big bowl with water then added ice and brought it back to him. "Put your foot in here."

He did as she instructed and groaned. "I thought you were training to heal the sick, not torture them." He gave her a suspicious glare. "Is this some kind of payback?"

Maggie winked at him. "You ride on black diamond trails; you pay the price."

Colin grunted. "I thought I'd at least get a little sympathy from you."

"After all these years, you should know better than that."

His gaze moved to the hallway that led to her bedroom, then back to her. "So, I was right."

She hated his gloating expression, but she couldn't deny the truth. "Yes."

"So, you and my brother hooked up."

Maggie cringed inwardly. She hated the term *hooked up*. It made what she and Daniel had sound crass and cheap.

"No, we did not *hook up*." Daniel leaned against the doorway, wearing nothing but a pair of jeans and a scowl. "We are involved, and we care about each other."

True and true. Maggie couldn't have said it better herself.

Colin met his brother's icy stare. "Don't get all huffy. It's just a term everyone uses."

Daniel's eyes narrowed. "Don't use it to describe us."

Colin's curious gaze darted between them. "It's about time you two figured out you were meant to be together." He shifted his foot. "How long do I leave it in here."

"Ten minutes then switch to heat," Maggie advised.

Colin groaned again.

"Quit your bellyaching," Daniel said. "This was self-inflicted. You wanna play rough, you gotta expect some injuries. If you were already in the Big Leagues, you wouldn't have Maggie around to take care of you."

Colin had been drafted by Seattle in the first round as a shortstop, and he'd leave as soon as he finished the semester. She just hoped this injury didn't change that.

"Maggie has never been my nursemaid. I'd bet if you ask her, she'd tell you she only got me the ice water so she wouldn't have to listen to me whine."

"You got that right." Maggie's stomach grumbled in the intervening silence and brought hearty laughter from them both men.

"You are the only woman I know who has the metabolism of a hummingbird," Colin said.

Maggie grinned and shrugged. "It's out of my control."

Daniel stepped into the kitchen. "Why don't I whip something up?"

"I'd love that, except I'm already late for class. I'll grab something later." Maggie turned for the bedroom to dress.

Daniel slipped an arm around her and gave her a kiss that made her wish she had time to drag him back to bed.

He released her and she swayed a moment before collecting herself. "Go get ready while I make you something to take with you."

"What about me? I'm hungry, too," Colin broke in.

Daniel opened the refrigerator. "You're more than capable of cooking for yourself."

Colin held up his injured foot.

"Again, self-inflicted. Doesn't count." Daniel closed the refrigerator, grabbed a banana from the counter and tossed it to him.

"That won't fill me up."

The sound of their bickering and the steady thump of her heart followed her all the way to the bathroom. She'd taken a giant step getting involved with Daniel so quickly—something she'd never done with any of her other boyfriends. But her feelings for Daniel were different—deeper and more intense. If it didn't work out, she'd be heart broken, but what was life without risk?

~

MAGGIE DROVE Daniel to the airport a week later—a bittersweet farewell. She blinked back the tears pooling in her eyes. "Don't do anything stupid." Maggie tried for a flip tone, but her voice wavered and cracked.

Daniel cradled her in his arms. "I'm going to be okay, Maggie."

She pushed back, her body rigid. "You don't know that. Don't make promises you can't keep."

He pressed her head to his chest. "I promise I will come back to torment you."

She said nothing for the longest time, just listened to the steady beat of his heart beneath her ear. Finally she said, "I'm holding you to that."

Laughter rumbled through his chest. He trailed a finger over her cheek.

Her breath caught. Their eyes met, and she leaned in close.

The intensity of his gaze shook her to her core. "I'm going to miss you, Maggie Murphy. Will you wait for me?"

"As in sit at the apartment and spend all my time thinking about you?"

More laugher. "Hardly. I meant will you be my girlfriend and tell all the other guys to take a hike?"

Her breath caught and her heart stuttered. "I could, so long as you disband your harem."

He stared deep into her eyes. "They were gone the instant I had you."

Tears pooled in her eyes again. "You know just how to make a girl melt in your arms."

"Does that mean you'll wait for me?"

Maggie nodded, unable to get the words out.

"I'll miss you."

Maggie tightened her arms around him, then released him. "Go out there and show them Daniel Gregorio has what it takes."

Daniel's voice cracked. "This is what I love about you. You always shoot to be the best and expect the same for those around you."

An announcement came over the loudspeakers. "Flight 2294 is now boarding."

"That's me, and I've still got to get through security." He kissed her one last time, then sprinted to the stairs. "Email me," he called over his shoulder.

She watched him take the stairs two at a time, then disappear from sight, leaving her stunned, lonely, and excited about his new adventure all at once.

He'd said he loved her. No, he'd said that's what he loved about her. Not quite the same thing, but close. They'd started something special, and she had to still the urge to rush in headlong. She wanted to give what had developed time to flourish and grow, and just maybe it would become more with the right nurturing, or maybe it wouldn't. A long distance relationship wasn't easy to maintain and only time would tell if they could make it work.

Maggie headed back to the car, pride swelling inside her. Daniel was undertaking something few men or women got an opportunity to do. And while she'd teased him about his athletic abilities, that's all it had been—teasing. He was a gifted athlete—a winner. He would make the team, of that she had no doubt, and she was eager to begin her own journey with the World Health Center. Working for WHC gave her the opportunity to make a difference in the world by providing medical care to people in desperate need.

Eagerness pulsed through her as she left the airport. In just a few weeks she'd be embarking on her own journey, and Daniel had given her the perfect sendoff—him. Life was damn good.

~

PRESENT DAY...

Maggie surfaced, the water whisking her down the canyon, ripping up trees and boulders in its wake.

Maggie scrambled for solid ground. She reached for a tree, but the water uprooted it, then swung it around. A branch slapped her face, the rough bark scraping her cheek. She barely missed smashing into another tree.

Snagging a low-hanging tree branch, she pulled herself up. When she finally reached the trunk, she wrapped her legs and arms around it as the water thundered past. She searched for Lightning, but couldn't see him. He was a strong swimmer, she reminded herself. He probably had a better chance of survival than she did, but it didn't stop her heart from clenching in fear.

Breathe Mags. You know what to do.

Colin's voice came to her as clearly as if he were beside her. She drew in a deep breath and recalled her training.

First step—avoid heat loss. She pulled herself higher so she was completely out of the water. Shivers wracked her body. The lightweight, quick-drying clothes were a plus, but it was still November and the water was cold. She searched for a way to solid ground, but all she saw was the deafening rush of the water hurling past her.

The tree shifted.

Crack! The roots snapped. An instant later, the churning mass of water swallowed her.

4

Rain pounded the van as Daniel and MD headed to Pine Ridge. The dark, angry clouds matched Daniel's mood as his thoughts kept circling back to Colin's broken body.

Never give up, never surrender.

The T-shirt Colin wore that last day. Why didn't the words give him comfort? Why couldn't he have saved his brother?

MD swore a string of epithets as Daniel hit a pothole jarring them both. "That pothole was the size of Lake Serenity."

Daniel grunted his agreement as he maneuvered the van through the driving wind and rain.

"You know, I've always appreciated your gift of gab."

Daniel choked out a laugh. "Still the king of understatement."

MD smiled, a devious twinkle lighting his eyes. "It's my signature statement." His voice took on a serious undertone. "I hope to God no one is out in this shit."

Daniel had the same thought, but he wasn't banking on it.

He avoided another pothole that was nearly as bad as the ambulance ride through Eastern Europe the time he'd nearly lost Maggie to rebel gunfire.

~

EIGHT YEARS AGO...

Daniel took out his cell phone and punched in Maggie's number. She answered on the first ring.

"Hey, you."

Just hearing her voice soothed away all the lonely nights they'd been apart. "Guess where I'm headed."

Her *harrumph* came back loud and clear, but he also heard the thread of excitement. "You know I hate surprises. Where are you going?"

Her zest for adventure was another thing he loved about her, the way she embraced life with open arms. "Eastern Europe."

"That's a big area. Maybe I'll see you there."

What the hell did that mean? "How would you do that?"

"Well, since we talked last, I'm in Poldivia."

Poldivia, a tiny Slavic country wedged between Slovenia and Croatia. The most volatile area in the region and precisely where his team was headed, but he couldn't tell her that because all their missions were top secret.

"That's a dangerous area."

"So I've heard from several people lately."

Silence followed her brief statement.

Most likely she'd been getting pressure from her family to come home, and while he understood their concerns, he also knew she was more than capable of taking care of herself.

"There's a lot of need here. I'm doing something important, I'm making a difference," she continued.

The enthusiasm in her voice warmed him to his core. They both had that primal desire to help others, to make a difference in the world.

"There's been an outbreak of tuberculosis here, and we're trying to get it under control. Oh Daniel, I feel like I've been searching my whole life for this. Does that make sense?"

It did. "You've found your calling."

"Oh my God, that's it exactly. How come you get it and no one else does?"

He was silent a moment. "I think you have to have a calling to understand when someone else has found theirs."

"Like you being in the military."

It was a statement not a question. "Yes. Can I assume your family hasn't been supportive?" he asked.

Maggie gave a grunt filled with exasperation. "The understatement of the year."

"Honestly, that was my gut reaction." He paused, debating how to proceed, but they'd always been honest with each other so he forged ahead. "I don't want you in danger. I don't know what I'd do if I lost you."

"I feel the same way about you being in the military, but I realized that you could survive all your missions, come home, and die in a car accident. So I decided to accept you for who you are for however long I have you."

Daniel was torn between desperately wanting to tell her to go home or at least leave the region for her safety, but he also knew doing so would put a wedge between them. "I'll find a way to deal with my fear just as you've done."

He checked the time. "I've gotta go." He hesitated again. "I wanted to tell you this in person, but it's more important that I tell you now. I love you, Maggie. Go do good in the world."

Her voice quavered. "I love you, too, but saying it doesn't begin to tell you how much you mean to me. You support me even when your instinct is to protect. That's—I don't know how to explain what I'm feeling, but it's everything. Be safe and come back to me."

"You do the same."

He disconnected the call. Elation warred with trepidation, the same as when he headed out on a mission. No wonder he loved her more than life itself.

～

DANIEL ARRIVED in Poldivia a week later. Everyone was jumpy and on edge as they waited for orders. Sitting still was not in their makeup, but they did it and did it well.

Rather than play cards with his team members, Daniel went through his medical supplies, checking to make sure he had everything he needed.

As he unzipped the pack, his thoughts turned to Maggie. What was she doing? Was she safe?

He pushed the last thought aside. He'd go crazy if he lingered on that.

MD sat down beside him. "Worrying about Maggie?"

A shiver crept over his spine whenever MD read his thoughts. "I still say you're psychic."

Raspy laughter rumbled from MD. "I just pay attention to detail. When you do, it's easy to read people. So, was I right?"

"Are you going to tell me I shouldn't be worried?" Daniel countered rather than answer his question.

"Hell no. I'd be scared shitless if she were my girl."

Daniel drew in a deep breath, then admitted, "Thinking about her messes with my head. I need to focus on the mission."

"And you will once we're actually moving. Waiting is making everyone nuts. You think about things you wouldn't think about if you weren't just sitting on your ass."

MD had a point. Waiting made him tense and anxious. "So have you heard anything?"

"Only what you've heard. We're taking down a group of rebels that plan to overthrow the Poldivian government."

Ryan Steen, the youngest in their unit dubbed The Kid, stuck his head in the tent. "It's time to rock and roll, girls. Briefing in ten minutes."

Leave it to The Kid to treat this like a party—due in part to his age and inexperience, but also his farm-boy naiveté. It was also why there was an instinctive need from the team to protect him.

Daniel and MD grabbed their gear and followed The Kid out of the tent.

THEY TOOK down the group with no injuries to the team and brought back the two rebels who'd survived the firefight. They turned them over to the CIA and were about to head out when a call came in that fighting had broken out in the southern region, trapping aid workers evacuating Tuzia—Maggie's aid station.

Tension coiled through him. These situations escalated rapidly. The aid workers could be dead before help arrived—*Maggie* could already be dead.

From the instant Daniel climbed onto the helicopter he was as taut as a rattler ready to strike.

MD clamped a hand on his shoulder. "Take a breath. Panicking won't help her or the rest of us. We're all here for you, and we're all going to get her out safe and sound."

Daniel clamped down the fear that had his head spinning and studied his team. MD was right. They were all ready and willing to risk their lives for Maggie and her group. Confidence replaced his fear. With his team behind him, they were invincible, and he stood a fighting chance of saving Maggie.

No one messed with his woman—no one.

THEY ARRIVED at the outskirts of Tuzia under full darkness. A pair of vans marked with red crosses were pinned down taking heavy gunfire. The imaginary rattler reared back to life hissing and spitting and itching for a fight.

It took every bit of restraint to keep Daniel from racing headlong into the hail of gunfire, and he still might have if Sloan and MD hadn't held him back. Instead, he strapped on the medical bag and gripped his rifle.

Hawk's gaze zeroed in on him. "You look tighter than a banjo spring about to snap, Gregorio. This isn't the time to play cowboy and go off half-cocked. If you can't rein in your emotions, I'll leave you here."

Daniel's hands clenched around the riffle. No fucking way he was being left behind.

"You hear me, Gregorio?"

Daniel grunted a response that could be interpreted as either a yes or no.

Hawk's dark gaze fixed on him a moment longer before he turned to MD and Sloan. "Keep him in line."

"Yes, sir," they said simultaneously.

"Move out." Hawk waved them forward, and Sloan and MD flanked him, their guns at the ready as they moved away from the chopper.

Bullets sprayed the dirt in front of them. Every instinct urged Daniel to run straight for the vehicles, but he corralled the impulse and stayed with his team, returning fire as they took cover in a stand of trees.

MD's voice crackled in their ears. "Two down, ten to go."

They zigzagged toward the rescue workers, dodging bullets, and continuing to fire at the rebels.

Fifty yards out, Hawk took a hit.

Daniel dropped down beside him. Sloan materialized out of the darkness to assist. They each grabbed an arm and pulled him behind the vehicle. They laid him on the ground, and Daniel checked the wound while Sloan and MD provided cover fire.

A through-and-through to the shoulder, no vital organs hit. Before Daniel could open his bag, a roll of gauze was thrust into his hand.

He looked up to find Maggie beside him, an open first-aid kit at her feet. It was the most beautiful sight in the world to see her healthy and whole. Relief washed over him and left him weak. He quickly shook it off and focused on his job.

"We don't have a lot, but it should be enough to wrap it up."

Daniel shrugged out of his pack and handed it to her. "We have plenty of supplies in here." He took just long enough to touch her cheek and assure himself she was truly alive and well. "You scared ten years off my life today. Can't you find somewhere less dangerous to work?"

Maggie opened the pack and smacked more gauze into his outstretched palm. Her gaze lasered through him as surely as if she'd taken a knife to his gut. "I'm glad to see you've been staying out of danger, too."

Sarcasm. He deserved that. The instant the words had left his mouth he'd wanted to pull them back.

"Sorry."

"You should be. I've got a job to do, the same as you."

"But—"

"But what?" Maggie demanded. "But it's different because you're worrying about me this time?"

That was exactly what he'd been about to say.

"I'd keep my mouth shut if I were you," Hawk advised through gritted teeth as Daniel wrapped his shoulder. "You'll only stick your foot in deeper."

Daniel's gaze shifted to Maggie, and he saw determination and anger smoldering in her eyes.

"Take the man's advice. You won't regret it."

"I've missed you," Daniel said instead.

Her eyes softened. "I've missed you, too."

"If you two love birds are done, how about finishing up so we can get the hell out of here," Hawk growled.

Daniel finished wrapping the wound and helped Hawk up. Hawk immediately spoke into his com. "Have we got an exit plan?"

"Take these bastards out," MD said.

"Let's load up."

"Can't do that, boss. They blew out the tires on both the vehicles," MD said.

"Our bird's taking fire, so we're hoofing it to the next extraction point. What other transportation options do we have?" Hawk asked.

"There's an ambulance, but we left it behind because it wouldn't start," Maggie said.

"Razor, take The Kid and get that thing running."

"We're on it, boss."

"If anyone can get it going, The Kid can. He spent his life on the farm and he can work magic on machines," Daniel assured her.

Maggie nodded. "We have another problem. We have two injured."

"How serious?" Hawk asked.

"The flesh wound is mobile, but our doc took a wound to the upper leg," Maggie said.

"Have you got a stretcher?" Hawk asked Maggie.

"In the back of the van."

Hawk turned to Daniel. "Get their doc loaded and ready to move on my command."

A bullet whizzed past Daniel as he got the stretcher from the back. With Maggie's help, they loaded her colleague onto the stretcher. Daniel waved to the other two aid workers crouched behind the van to follow them.

"Razor, what's your status?" Hawk asked.

"ETA two minutes."

Daniel spoke into his com. "We're ready,"

Hawk's voice came back to him. "Get the injured and the aid workers to the ambulance. We'll be covering your six."

Daniel and Sloan picked up the stretcher, and Maggie and her coworkers followed. "Keep low," Daniel told them.

They had to slow their pace to accommodate the aid workers, but they reached the ambulance. "Stay here," Daniel ordered Maggie and her group. He and Sloan headed back to cover their team members.

Once the rest of the team arrived, they set off. Daniel treated some minor injuries on his team while Maggie stayed with the injured doctor. He was headed to her when the van hit a pothole and lurched sharply to the left.

"I need help," Maggie shouted.

Daniel quickly moved to her side. "What happened?"

"She started hemorrhaging after we hit that pothole."

"I need light."

Maggie held a flashlight for him.

Blood soaked the floor.

"It's the femoral artery. Probably tore it when we hit the pothole."

Daniel applied a tourniquet and packed the wound.

Maggie took her pulse. "It's getting stronger."

Once the bleeding was under control, Daniel said, "The bullet snapped the bone. I'm going to go ahead and put a splint on it."

Once he was finished, Daniel dropped back to the floor, the adrenaline surge gone and leaving him shaky. One of his teammates handed him an energy drink, and he took several swallows.

Maggie sat down beside him, and he offered her a drink. She wrinkled her nose. "No, thanks."

"Take a couple of sips."

She took a drink and scowled. "I'd rather have straight whiskey."

The Kid slapped a hand on the driver's shoulder. "That can be arranged, right MD?"

MD winked at her in the rearview mirror. "I'll provide the finest money can buy."

Laughter erupted.

Maggie shot Daniel a puzzled look, and he leaned down to whisper in her ear. "Never accept alcohol from Mad Dog unless you like the cheapest money can buy."

"Mad Dog?"

"MD stands for Mad Dog 20/20."

"Not Medical Doctor?"

Daniel hooted out a laugh. "No. He got the name because he prefers cheap, rotgut liquor, and in particular, Mad Dog 20/20. He also turns into a mad dog whenever he drinks it."

She looked at their driver, then back at Daniel. "Really, I would have never guessed."

"Yeah, his transformation is a lot like a human into a werewolf."

"Hey, I'm not that bad," MD protested.

"You keep telling yourself that, but I've got the video to prove it."

MD grunted as laughter filled the ambulance.

Silence fell between them.

Maggie blew out a breath. "If I didn't say it earlier, thank you for saving us. I..." Her voice wavered. "I thought it was the end."

Her body trembled against him as the events of the day caught up with her. Daniel cradled her in his arms and pressed her head to his chest. "You're okay."

Slowly, the quivering subsided, and her breathing evened out. The rocking of the vehicle lulled her to sleep, and Daniel held her close, grateful she was alive and unharmed.

But would he be there next time to save her?

~

AFTER DEBRIEFING, Daniel went in search of Maggie—they'd flown directly to Germany. He found her at the hospital with the doctor from the aid station. She smiled at him, and his heart melted into a puddle at her feet.

"Daniel, I'm so glad you're here. Jane has been asking to see you."

The doctor held out a hand to him, and he shook it. "Jane Grant."

"Daniel Gregorio."

"So you're the medic who saved me."

"I had a little help from your colleague." Daniel gestured to Maggie.

Jane gave him a weak smile. "From what I see, you two make a good team."

Daniel concurred.

"Thank you, and please extend my thanks to your team for rescuing us. Things escalated faster than we anticipated."

"I will."

Maggie hugged her friend and told her she'd be back later, then accompanied Daniel out of the room.

They reached the elevator, and Daniel pushed the button to the lobby. The instant the door closed, he swept her in his arms and kissed her. Hot, insistent need throbbed within him. Only the ding of the elevator doors yanked them apart.

"Is there somewhere private we can go?" Maggie asked as they exited the hospital.

A woman after his own heart. No, correction. She already controlled that. He dangled a hotel key.

She grabbed it and hailed a cab.

"A woman who takes charge."

She flashed him a wicked smile. "No complaints. You knew what you were getting."

He had, and he'd gone after exactly what he'd wanted.

A taxi pulled up to the curb, and he opened the door for Maggie.

"Where to?"

Daniel gave the cabbie the name of the hotel. Twenty minutes later they were inside his room, and he was busily stripping off Maggie's clothes when his phone buzzed.

MD.

"What?" Daniel barked.

"We left a gift for you two on the table."

Daniel found a bottle of champagne. "What? No Mad Dog?"

"I tried but Sloan said, and I quote, 'No fuckin' way.'"

Daniel laughed. "Thanks."

"Quit gabbing and open that bottle."

"Hooah!"

The echo of five Hooahs came over the phone before he disconnected the call.

Disappointment filled her eyes. "Are you leaving?"

Daniel grabbed the bottle and glasses. "Nope. The boys left us a surprise."

Maggie bounced on the balls of her feet. "Champagne."

He popped the cork and poured them each a glass, then tapped his flute to hers. "To a successful mission."

Her eyes softened and turned dewy.

He ached with need for her, but instead of rushing her, he turned on the music, took her in his arms, and swayed to the ballad coming from the speakers.

She set her glass down and threaded her fingers through his hair.

"Daniel, it's been five months since we were together. I want you —now."

His arms tightened around her. "You read my mind."

"Hooah."

~

PRESENT DAY...

Daniel gripped the steering wheel as the wind swayed the van. He dodged another pothole and wished he could go back to those early days with Maggie. Life had been so simple even though they'd spent more time apart than together. Maybe distance did make the heart grow fonder.

"There's the turnoff." MD pointed to the Pine Ridge entrance.

Flashing lights cut through the rain. Easing off the gas pedal, Daniel turned into the parking area, wove around the emergency vehicles, and parked at the end of the lot.

"Let's go find out where they need us," Daniel said.

"Hopefully anywhere but sitting around."

Daniel nodded in agreement as he pulled up the hood of his jacket and got out of the van. He spoke into his ear bud to Sloan. "Any word from Maggie?"

"Nope. Still going to voicemail."

"Keep trying."

Uneasiness burned in his gut. Where the hell was she?

5

Maggie groaned, her body battered and bruised, but she was alive and on dry ground. The water disappeared as rapidly as it arrived, leaving her very much alone and lost in the wilderness.

She whistled for Lightning, praying for a miracle, but no dog bounded toward her, in fact the only sound was the echo of her voice. She whistled again and waited. Nothing.

Maggie dropped her backpack on the ground and plopped down beside it. Miraculously, she hadn't lost it, and other than a few scrapes that stung like the devil, she had no serious injuries.

She opened the backpack to see what had survived the raging waters. Her phone still functioned thanks to the waterproof case, but she didn't have cell service. She shut it down and restarted it to see if she could pick up better service.

While she waited for it to restart, she found a half dozen nutritional bars, a pair of gloves, hat and wool socks, all soggy, a map, a first-aid kit that had a couple of Band-Aids, antibacterial cream, and some gauze, and last, a battered banana that didn't look the least bit appetizing.

The phone came back up and still no service. She sent a nine-one-one text, hoping at some point it would go through if she got service, then tucked it back into the pack, and studied the sky. Still plenty of daylight to make it down to her car. She pushed to her feet, her legs shaky and weak. She peeled the banana and forced it down since it would only turn to mush in her pack.

Within minutes the shaking subsided. She judiciously sipped the water from her pack, just in case she had to spend the night in the wilderness.

She'd done it before, but never alone and never without sufficient supplies. She'd assisted in plenty of survival training classes at Adventure Docs, but she'd always had Daniel and the team there as backup. This time she was on her own.

Where was her knight in shining armor when she needed him?

~

Six years ago...

Maggie's cell rang. Colin's name scrolled across the screen, and she answered the call. "Perfect timing."

"Where are you?"

"On a bus, headed home for the holidays. Where are you?"

"Still in this sweltering hell hole."

His comment drew a smile from her. He'd walked away mid-season from a lucrative professional baseball contract to join the Army—specifically the Rangers. He'd felt an obligation to serve his country after the latest string of terrorist attacks. Unfortunately for Colin he'd gone straight from boot camp to the Middle East, and he was currently serving his second tour. He hated the heat, the sand—pretty much the entire climate. He missed the lush forests, mild summers, and even the cold winters of home.

While he might hate the climate, he loved the military. A true adventure junkie, Colin thrived on the training and missions, he lived and breathed the *be all you can be.*

"How much longer will you be there?"

"Damned if I know. What about you? When are you done in Poldivia?"

"Another six months, then I'm not sure what I'll do. When's your next leave?"

"I don't know. All leaves have been suspended for the immediate future."

Her breath caught. "Why, what's happened?"

Silence.

"Colin, your silence scares me more than whatever you're holding back."

"I assume you haven't seen the news or read a paper in the past few days."

"No, I've barely had phone service. Why?"

His ragged breathing filled the momentary pause. "A bomb blast took out a city block yesterday. Hundreds of civilians were killed, plus a group of soldiers on leave."

"Daniel?" She barely pushed the words out, the knot in her throat threatening to strangle her.

"No, he's fine, but one of my friends didn't make it."

She slumped back against the seat. "I'm so sorry. How are you?" A lame question, but she didn't know what else to say.

Another longer silence that told Maggie all wasn't well. How could it be?

Colin's voice cracked. "She had kids, Maggie. She was out celebrating her thirtieth birthday. I was supposed to be with them, but Daniel called and I told her I'd catch up. Her kids won't have a mom for Christmas." His voice broke. "No kid should have to go through that."

Maggie's chest ached. They—she, Colin, and Daniel—had seen too much death. "If I could, I'd fly to be with you."

"I know and I appreciate that, but I don't want you here."

She drew in a sharp breath. "Don't you dare tell me it's too dangerous."

Colin released a weary sigh. "I didn't mean that. I meant I don't want you to see the things I've seen. You know I support what you do, don't you?"

Exasperation metamorphosed to guilt. "Yes, I do and I'm sorry. I shouldn't have made that assumption."

"It's okay. I know you get a lot of pressure from your family," Colin said.

The understatement of the year. The pressure from her parents and siblings to come home was relentless.

"I gotta go, Mags. I'll call when I can."

"Watch your back."

"Always."

Long after they hung up, their conversation stayed with her. After he left the military, would there be anything left of that sweet boy she loved like a brother?

~

MAGGIE ARRIVED in Paradise Falls on the coattails of a major winter storm that left the town awash in the miracle of virgin snow—a pure pristine white that clung to rooftops, sidewalks and long, sweeping branches on the pine trees.

Her mother had decorated the house to Martha-Stewart perfection with a massive tree, lights, and the scent of pumpkin and cloves filling every room. Truly the white Christmas she'd been longing for. The only thing missing to make it a perfect holiday was to have Colin and Daniel home.

Grabbing a cup of holiday-spiced coffee from the kitchen, Maggie stood before the woodstove to warm her backside while she called Daniel. She'd have preferred the privacy of her room, but cell service was better downstairs.

Sloan answered. "About time you checked in. Lover boy has been pacing for the last hour."

"It's Maggieeee," Sloan called out as if he were in the third grade.

"Give me the damn phone before I make you wish you'd never been born."

Maggie smiled, envisioning a game of keep away going on at the other end between Daniel and Sloan.

She heard more squabbling, then the slamming of a door. "Maggie, are you still there?"

"I'm here. Are you alone?"

"Yes. I just booted out Sloane and MD."

She pictured those two with their ears pressed to the door. "Are you sure they're not eavesdropping or peeking through the window?"

He snorted. "There are no guarantees with those two. But I don't care if they hear us."

Maggie absorbed the heat from the woodstove. "Aw, you miss me."

"Of course I do."

She fluttered her eyelashes as if he could see her. "Tell me how much."

"Enough to chuck my career and follow you to the far corners of the earth like a lovesick puppy."

There was such sincerity in his voice that she believed him. "Not necessary. We'll see each other soon enough and make up for lost time."

His voice turned raspy. "What exactly do you have in mind?"

Maggie's burst of laughter drew a raised eyebrow from her father sitting at the table reading the paper. "I can give you generalities."

"You're not alone."

"Afraid not, and no promises how long my connection will hold. The snow storm is wreaking havoc on the cell service here."

"Okay, so what do you have in mind next time we meet?"

Her face warmed, and it had nothing to with the heat from the fire. "Well, you could start by cooking me dinner."

"You want to waste time eating?"

"It's called sustenance, and a girl's gotta eat."

"I swear food always comes first with you."

She smiled, and yearned for some time alone with him to prove that wasn't always true. "Close, but there are some exceptions. Now, if you'll quit interrupting me, you might discover I have some suggestions that interest you." When he said nothing, she dropped her voice and continued. "I'm thinking we start with dessert—strawberries loaded with whipped cream."

"You're planning on sharing this dessert, aren't you?"

His question came off like a dare and sent shivers chasing over her skin. "Absolutely."

Daniel smacked his lips, and her laughter drew another curious look from her father, but he buried his face in the paper.

"I miss you—miss you so much I ache. When are we going to actually see each other?"

Daniel's voice turned tender. "I'm working on it."

"Work faster," she whispered.

"*Oh Daniel, I miss you soooo much,*" Sloan and MD echoed from beyond the door.

"I'm going to kick your asses," Daniel yelled, and got very loud lip smacking sounds in response. "There is no privacy here."

"Same here."

A beat of silence.

"I love you," she said, "and tell those juvenile bozos they're just jealous because they don't have a woman like me."

Daniel's laughter warmed her through and through. "Wait, you have to hear their response before you go."

She heard the door open and bodies stumbling. "Maggie says to tell you that you're behaving like horny teenagers because you're jealous you don't have a woman like her."

Maggie heard muttering, and something to the effect of "I hate smart women," and "we were only teasing."

The resounding slam of the door had Maggie pulling the phone from her ear. "Maybe that was too harsh."

"Harsh is the only language they understand."

"Well, be the better man and show some compassion since you have me and they don't have anyone."

Daniel blew out a breath like a little boy reprimanded for being unkind. "Okay, but be warned, I'm finding us some one-on-one time without anyone interfering."

"Any chance that will be during Christmas?"

"I wish."

The longing in his voice matched the yearning in her heart. "I love you."

"Love you more."

She ended the call, loneliness slipping over her even though she was surrounded by love and warmth. It just wasn't the same without Daniel at her side.

Her dad made a pretense of rattling the paper as he folded it up and put it in the basket her mother used for recycling. "I'd best get the sidewalks shoveled. Could use some help."

Maggie tucked the phone in her back pocket and took her coat from the hook, following her dad to the garage. They shoveled in companionable silence, the quiet enveloping Maggie like a soothing hug.

"So you and Daniel seem to be pretty serious."

Maggie scooped a shovel full of snow and threw it off to the side, then stopped and stared at her dad. "Why do I get the feeling there's more behind that statement?"

He leaned on the shovel handle, looked at the sky as if gauging the weather, then Maggie. "Let's just say I have concerns."

"About Daniel or that we're dating?"

"A little of both. I know you've had your eye on him for a long time."

She saw no point in denying what was the truth so she gave a slow nod.

"You two are very different."

"So are you and Mom."

"We have our differences, but our fundamental beliefs are similar."

Maggie watched her dad unzip his coat and lay it over the fence. "And you think Daniel and I don't have that?"

He shook his head. "I couldn't say. I just think when a woman sets her sights on a man she ought to make sure, that's all. And when that woman is my daughter, I don't want to see her heart broken."

Maggie put a hand on his arm. "Heart break is a part of life."

"It is, but that doesn't mean I want to see my girl suffer."

He slipped an arm around her and pulled her close. "Do you love him?"

Maggie pressed a kiss to his cheek, then pulled back. "With all my heart."

"And he loves you, too?"

"He does."

He gave her another squeeze, then released her. "Okay then. I've said my piece. Better get this driveway shoveled before your mother has to leave."

That was what she loved most about her dad. He said what he had to say, then moved on.

"Why don't I shovel the walks while you run the snow blower?"

"Good idea."

Maggie's phone dinged while her dad fired up the snow blower. A text from her brother Liam.

Meet for coffee?

What time? She texted back.

An hour.

Where?

A minute later her phone dinged. *The usual. Mugs Coffee House.*

K.

She helped her dad finish up, then walked over to meet Liam. Christmas trees hung from the lamp posts up and down Main Street, their blinking lights visible against the dark clouds. Shop windows were decorated with lights and tinsel, and wreaths hung on every door.

She reached Mugs. A huge coffee cup was painted in the window with a candy cane in it. She pushed open the door and found Liam at their usual booth nursing a cup of coffee and eating a bagel.

She slid in across from him. "Did you order me anything?" She'd barely gotten the words out when a waitress set a steaming cup of coffee and a lightly toasted bagel in front of her.

Maggie flashed her a grin. "Thank you." While she added cream to her coffee, she sized up her brother. "You're never this thoughtful. Who died?"

Liam clutched his chest in mock pain. "Can't a guy do something nice for his baby sister?"

His sparkling green eyes appeared guileless, but she knew better. "I was teasing, but you did have a purpose for inviting me here, didn't you?"

He stirred his coffee, then clanked the spoon against the rim. "I see why Daniel's got a thing for you. He likes direct women."

His eyes locked with hers and she read uncertainty in the green depths. That was not something she associated with her older brother. Instead of pressing him, she waited.

Perplexed, Maggie watched her brother fidget. Also totally out of character. Liam Murphy never squirmed. There was more going on here than he was saying.

"I'm going to open my own microbrewery," he blurted out finally.

"All of this drama over a microbrewery. It sounds great, so what's the problem?"

"Mom and Dad. They won't like that I'm chucking my career for something risky."

Maggie smeared huckleberry jam over her bagel then broke off a piece and chewed as she considered his comment. She swallowed, then sipped her coffee. "What makes you so sure? I mean honestly, it's not like accounting was ever your calling."

Liam puffed up, offended. "It's a perfectly acceptable career that gives me a steady income."

Maggie sized him up. "Who are you trying to convince, me or you?"

His indignation deflated, he slumped back against the worn vinyl. "I don't know. Me, I guess."

Maggie stared at him over the rim of her coffee cup. "You want to know what I think?"

"Not really."

"Too bad." She added more cream to her coffee and stirred it, then pointed her spoon at him. "You shouldn't have invited me here and spilled your guts if you didn't want my opinion. This has nothing to do with Mom and Dad's reaction. This is all about you. You want to do this, but you're scared to give up your stable, secure job to try it."

Liam's tone took on a defensive edge. "So what if I am? I could lose everything. I could hate it."

Maggie inched up a shoulder. "You could, or you could be outrageously happy and successful. You won't know until you try."

The tension eased from him and amusement danced in his eyes. "So, you'll wash dishes for me?"

She sniffed. "Not likely. I won't be your slave, but I will serve beer and bus tables when I'm home."

He spread cream cheese over his bagel. "When are you coming home—for good?"

She'd been asked this question by everyone. At least he hadn't started with it. She offered up her pat response. "I have another six months in Poldivia. I haven't decided what I'll do after that."

Liam's hand closed over hers. "I understand you've got to do this, but I miss you."

No pressure. No come home where it's safe, which made her want to dig her heels in and keep doing what she was doing. In truth, she missed Paradise Falls and her family.

"Thank you. I miss you, too, I miss all of this."

"So, why are you staying away?"

She wished she had an answer to that. "I'm making a difference. These people need me."

Liam saw through her glib response recognizing it for what it was —an excuse. "You could do plenty of good right here—why do you need to be on the other side of the world?"

Liam's words stayed with her all the way to their parents' house, and she still didn't have an answer. After the aid station had been overrun, and Daniel came to the rescue, she'd been ready to pack up and come home for good. Only Colin's jeer from childhood, *bawk, bawk, bawk,* had kept her from tucking her tail between her legs and racing for home.

She wasn't a quitter, but maybe it was time for a change.

~

MAGGIE STEPPED into her skis at Dover Point trail Christmas Eve morning. Snow drifted over her as soft as the flutter of butterfly wings. She paused to absorb the absolute silence of the moment. Peace settled over her as she set off.

Someone had already broken trail, so she followed the tracks. The only sound was the swish of her skis and her breathing as the trail took a steep, upward incline. She'd come out looking for a workout that made her forget about missing Daniel and the fact that he wouldn't be with her for Christmas, and she'd found it.

She followed the trail high above Paradise Falls and stopped at the shelter where a few coals smoldered in the fire pit. She tossed a log on the fire and stared out over Paradise Falls. The sun momentarily broke through the clouds, allowing a brief view of the tiny, snow-capped town below. Another tug of homesickness twisted through her.

It's time, Maggie.

She blew out a frosty breath. Change never came easy for her. She loved the people she worked with, the families she'd helped, but it was time to admit the truth. She wanted to come home, put down roots, and build a life here.

She held her hands out over the flame and absorbed the warmth as cold settled in her body. She wanted to build a life with Daniel here in Paradise Falls, but he'd made no indication he was ready to make a change, so the question was would she be happy in Paradise Falls without him at her side?

Who was she kidding? She'd never had Daniel at her side. In fact, in the three years they'd been together their relationship amounted to stolen weekends and a few extended vacations. And while she'd loved the passion and excitement between them, she was ready for more than an adrenaline rush. She wanted a home, marriage, and children.

Maggie stared down at the town below hoping for a sign that she was making the right decision, but she felt nothing other than the longing to come home.

She left the shelter and headed back to her parents' house with new purpose. Indecision no longer weighed her down. She was ready to come home. How that impacted her relationship with Daniel, she didn't know, but she loved him and would find a way to make it work.

She spent the rest of the day helping her mother prepare food for the Christmas Eve gathering with her siblings and friends, that included Tom Gregorio, Colin and Daniel's father.

Noah and Sarah arrived first with Jessica and Matt. Her nephew was already a teenager and her niece wasn't far behind. Wasn't it just yesterday they'd been babies?

She hugged them, then squeezed Sarah tight. She pulled back to study her face. "You never age. What's your secret?"

Her smile looked forced, brittle. "Nothing special."

Maggie looped an arm through hers and whispered conspiratorially. "There's hot buttered rum in the kitchen. Care to join me for a cup?"

Sarah's smile widened. "Count me in."

She'd just poured them each a mug when Liam called from the living room.

"Maggie, your Christmas present just arrived."

Perplexed, she looked at Sarah who shrugged and sipped her toddy.

Jessica raced into the kitchen, her eyes gleaming with excitement. "Aunt Maggie, you've got to come see this." She grabbed her hand and pulled her toward the living room.

Sarah trailed after them carrying Maggie's hot toddy while sipping her own.

Was that a smile she was hiding behind her mug? What was going on?

Jessica clasped her hands together and bounced on the balls of her feet when they entered the dining room. "Close your eyes, Aunt Maggie!"

Maggie put her hands on her hips feigning exasperation. "What is going on?"

"Pleeeease close your eyes."

She couldn't deny her niece, especially when she was so obviously excited, so she closed her eyes.

Jessica took her hand and led her toward the living room, the sudden silence unnerving. The Murphy house was never quiet.

"Can I open my eyes?"

"No!" exploded from the entire room.

"What is going—"

"Always were impatient."

Maggie's eyes flew open and there wrapped in a giant red bow stood Daniel. She blinked to make sure he was really there. Tears flooded her eyes as she flung herself into his arms.

"You told me you were on a mission, that you wouldn't be home for Christmas."

His arms slipped around her, squeezing her securely against his chest. "I was and I didn't think we would be done in time, but we finished early."

"Why didn't you call me?"

He gently wiped the tears from her cheeks. "I wanted to surprise you and with the weather as it is, I didn't want to disappoint you in case I couldn't get here. You can thank your brother for getting me here." He gestured to Liam. "He drove all the way to Spokane to pick me up."

She eyed her brother. "Did everyone know about this but me?"

"Of course."

"And the ribbon was your idea, too?" she asked her brother.

Liam shot her a megawatt grin. "I thought it was appropriate."

She gave Daniel a dubious look. "And you agreed with him?"

"I kind of got wrapped up in the idea."

A collective groan went around the room.

"Okay, a really a bad pun." He leaned in close to whisper in her ear. "I was actually hoping you'd want to unwrap me when we were alone."

His words sent pink rushing to her cheeks, and she gave him a warning glance to behave. "You know I'm an open presents Christmas morning kind of girl, but I might make an exception and open one present on Christmas eve—just this once."

The twinkle in his eyes said more than any words he could utter. "What about me? Do I get to open a present, too?"

Maggie shot him a saucy wink. "I have a feeling you might get lucky tonight."

"I'm banking on it."

"Enough private talk. Open your present, Maggie," Liam shouted out.

Maggie grabbed the end of the ribbon and pulled, then spun Daniel around unwinding the ribbon until he stood before her in snug jeans and a blue sweater that matched his eyes.

She clapped a hand to her mouth, the ribbon falling to the floor. "Oh my gosh it's Daniel!"

"You're under the mistletoe," Jessica squealed.

Daniel glanced above them, then down at Maggie. He slid an arm around her waist and drew her to him. "Merry Christmas," he murmured, then planted on kiss on her that stole her breath and brought a round of applause from the group.

~

PRESENT DAY...

Maggie might have divorced Daniel, but she'd made every moment she had with him count. She had plenty of regrets where he was concerned, but she didn't regret marrying him.

She pushed her way through the thick brush, wishing she hadn't lost her walking sticks in the water because it would have made it a lot easier. At least the foliage and trees blocked the wind, which helped keep her warm, but even so shudders left her quaking.

Her foot slipped on the slick, muddy ground, but she managed to stay upright. Any other time she might have considered this hike down the mountain a challenge, but cold, hungry, and exhausted, all she wanted was to get to her car.

She took out her phone again and checked for service.

Nothing, and the battery only had a bar left. She turned it off and tucked it back into her backpack.

The cold seeped into her, zapping her strength, but she focused on putting one foot in front of the other.

She whistled for Lightning again and refused to consider any alternative other than he would find her.

Snowflakes drifted from the sky and she groaned.

What more could possibly go wrong?

6

Daniel dialed Liam's cell as he and MD walked to the command center at Pine Ridge.

"Yeah."

Boisterous laughter and a round of boos echoed in the background.

"It's Daniel."

"What's up?"

"I'm looking for Maggie. Is she there?"

"No, I haven't seen her since the race yesterday. Is something up?"

"There's been some flash flooding, and we've been called in to help."

"She's not answering her cell?"

"No."

A long pause filled with shouts for another round.

Concern filled his voice. "She always answers her cell."

"I know." Another wave of trepidation swept over Daniel. "I'll call Noah and have him check the house."

"Keep me posted, and if you need help, I'll get someone to cover for me."

"Thanks. I'll call if we need more hands." Daniel ended the call and dialed Noah.

"Da!" Jon's screech overrode Noah's hello.

"Noah, it's Daniel."

"Sorry about that. Jon was playing with my phone when it rang. What's up?"

"Have you seen, Maggie?"

"No, why?"

"There's been some flash flooding, and we've been called in. She's not answering her cell or her landline. Could you go over and see if she's at the house and have her call Sloan?"

"Sure thing. Jon and I will run over there right now and call you back."

"Thanks."

Daniel dialed Maggie's cell and it went straight to voicemail. Urgency filled him. Something was wrong. Maggie always had her cell with her, always answered.

He stuffed the phone in his pocket.

"She's okay," MD said.

Daniel nodded, wishing MDs words reassured him, but they didn't. If he and Maggie were still married, he'd know where she was. How had something so good gone so wrong?

∼

Six years ago...

Daniel planned Maggie's Christmas gift down to the smallest detail. He didn't want anything to go wrong. He'd picked a resort just an hour out of Paradise Falls—a cabin on Moosehead Lake with all the amenities, including a huge fireplace and massive windows with views of the lake.

Daniel stood by the SUV he'd borrowed from Liam while he waited for Maggie to finish saying goodbye to her sister, Becky.

She came down the steps, her cheeks pink from the cold. She rushed forward, and flung herself into his arms, kissing him soundly.

"I'm so glad you got us this cabin."

Warmth filled him as he reached behind her and opened the car door. She thought the trip was her gift, but he had something more in mind.

She slid into the car. He closed the door and went around to the driver's side.

"So where are we going?"

"It's a surprise."

Her stomach rumbled as if on cue.

"Are you hungry?"

She arched a brow at him. "What a silly question? Of course I am. But the question you should be asking is whether I want to waste time eating or get to wherever we're going and have my way with you."

Daniel burst out laughing. "Okay, do you want to take time to eat or go to the cabin I rented and ravish me?" Her face glowed and her laughter told him all he needed to know. "I'm going to say you want me and room service."

"In that order," she confirmed.

"You may want to revise that plan since the cabin I rented is about an hour away."

"An hour if the roads aren't icy. I'll starve."

He handed her a granola bar. "I came prepared."

She tore open the wrapper. "Okay, this will tide me over for now, but I need real food when we get to the cabin, unless we can find somewhere private to pull over." She wiggled her eyebrows at him.

"I'll see what I can do."

The roads were plowed and clear all the way to the cabin. Instead of the restaurant Daniel had chosen, they opted for burgers at a tiny mom and pop burger joint and got them to go. Thirty minutes later they arrived and were finally settled in their cabin.

The instant the door shut behind them Daniel dropped the bags and Maggie looped her arms around his neck. "Okay Soldier Boy, show me what you've got."

And he did until he elicited a "Hooah" from her—not once but three times. And for good measure she brought a few out of him.

~

Daniel wanted this trip to be special—magical—and he'd pulled out all the stops to ensure it.

He'd made a reservation at the restaurant at the resort per Liam's recommendation, but at the last minute changed his mind. Instead, he took Maggie cross country skiing under a full moon.

"Where are we going?" Maggie asked.

"To a shelter that's supposed to have a view of the valley. There's even a spot for a bonfire. I packed a picnic while you were showering, and I thought we could ski up and have a late dinner."

"Oh, I love it!"

The sparkle in her eyes sent joy racing to his heart. "According to the desk clerk, the trail has lights all the way to the shelter and beyond if we want to ski farther."

"I can't wait. It sounds amazing."

And it was. The temperatures hovered in the teens, but the night was calm and perfect for Daniel's plan.

They reached the shelter as a group of people were leaving. Daniel added more wood to the fire.

Maggie turned in a circle her face alight with wonder. "This is amazing."

One of the many things he loved about Maggie—the way she embraced life with her whole heart—someone who experienced life like he did.

Unable to keep his hands off her, he spun her in a circle.

Her cheeks turned a deeper hue of pink and her eyes shone with an inner delight that he wanted to wrap himself in.

He twirled her one last time, then released her. He brushed the hair from her face. "I love you, Maggie Murphy. More than I thought I could ever love anyone. I can't imagine life without you by my side."

The fire warmed his backside as he dropped down on one knee and took the velvet box from his pocket. "Will you marry me?"

Tears gathered in her eyes as she pressed a hand to her lips. "Oh Daniel, it's beautiful." Her finger shook as she ran it over the marquee setting.

"Are you going to answer the boy?"

Daniel looked over his shoulder to see an older couple had just arrived.

The woman shushed her husband, but he waved her off.

Maggie held out her left hand and he slid on the ring. A perfect fit.

"Not much of an acceptance," the old man muttered. "Least you could do is kiss the boy."

Maggie tugged Daniel to his feet and did just that.

"Now there's a proper acceptance."

Daniel held up his thumb and the old man winked at him. "Aw, young love makes my heart go a pitty-pat."

Maggie's lips curved into a smile beneath his. "Maybe we could get him to officiate the wedding."

Daniel laughed. "Not likely. Your parents and my dad would kill us if we didn't have a full blown Catholic wedding."

Maggie sighed. "We could elope."

Daniel shook his head. "Not gonna happen. They'd never speak to us again if we did that."

Maggie nodded. "I know, but a girl can hope."

"Most women want the big wedding."

A wicked gleam filled her eyes as she shook a finger at him. "You should know by now I'm not most women."

Definitely not. She was one of kind, and the one woman in the world for him.

～

DANIEL HAD two days left of his leave and while he wanted to spend every minute with Maggie, he'd promised Colin he would look into his business idea that combined emergency medicine with adventure sports.

Asking Maggie to marry him had altered his career plans. Instead of reenlisting, he wanted a home and a life with her right here in Paradise Falls.

While he still loved the military, he wanted more than a few stolen moments with Maggie and the Adventure Docs plan would give him the best of both. Time with Maggie and a job that kept him active, not stuck behind a desk all day.

He made a dozen stops that included pricing equipment, talking to a real estate agent, and the bank for a potential loan. By the time he finished, he had a longer to-do list than when he started. Getting a new business up and running would take a lot of time and money, but he was up for the job.

When he finished, he found Maggie at Mugs Coffee House sipping a mocha and eating a bagel with Abby Sullivan, an old friend of her brother Noah's. She and her husband Jon were home for the holidays. They traveled extensively, but Daniel suspected their trips would decrease with the progression of Jon's ALS.

It took a powerful love to marry someone knowing they were in the early stages of ALS. His heart thumped against his chest as his eyes met Maggie's. Suddenly he understood a love that strong. He would do anything for Maggie—anything.

Abby's face brightened when she saw him. "Daniel, it's been years. So good to see you." She pushed back her chair. "Take my seat. I was just leaving."

"Don't rush off on my account."

Pain momentarily washed across her expression, then disappeared. "I need to get home." She turned to Maggie and hugged her. "It's so good to see you and congratulations. Let's get together when you're back in town. We should have the house finished by then."

She hugged Daniel, then hurried off.

"What house?" Daniel asked after ordering coffee and a bagel.

"They're building a house across from Noah and Sarah." Maggie's eyes filled with an emptiness he rarely saw. "Jon's travel days are about over."

Daniel stirred his coffee, fighting off a wave of injustice. "Life just isn't fair sometimes."

"It's not, but according to Abby, Jon is always upbeat and ready to face whatever life throws at him."

Daniel stared out the door where Abby had disappeared. "I can't imagine how difficult it must be to be his caretaker." He threaded his fingers through hers. "She must really love him."

Maggie stared at their entwined fingers. "It's funny, but I always thought it was Noah she loved, not Jon."

"Do you really think she'd marry Jon knowing he had ALS if she didn't love him?"

Maggie's eyes shot up to his. "Oh, she loves him, but I don't think it's romantic love. I know that Noah was in love with her when they were growing up."

"And then Sarah got pregnant."

Maggie nodded. "Did it seem strained between Sarah and Noah on Christmas Eve?"

"Yes, but it's seemed that way for a while to me."

"Me, too," Maggie whispered. "I hate seeing them unhappy."

Daniel tightened his fingers around hers. "There are some things that you can't fix, and this is one of them." He fingered her diamond. "So, did Abby like the ring?"

Radiance lit her face. "She loved it, and so do I if I forgot to tell you."

Her comment drew a laugh from him. "No, you didn't forget. You told me when I proposed, over dinner, on the way back to the cabin and you even showed me in private how much you loved it."

Her cheeks turned a rosy pink that heightened her color. He lowered his voice to a soft purr. "Your gratitude came through loud and clear. Care to find a private place and show me again?"

Maggie's color deepened. "I would love to, but I don't have anywhere private to take you."

He lifted her hand and kissed it. "I think our next order of business is to find a place of our own."

Maggie raised her mug and tapped it to his. "I like the sound of that."

~

PRESENT DAY...

He and Maggie had found the perfect house, and Daniel thought they'd start a family and grow old there. They'd made plenty of memories in that house that would stay with him forever.

Daniel tugged his coat tighter as the cool air penetrated his jacket.

"I hope to hell most of these cars are here for search and rescue," MD said.

Daniel's gaze swept the parking lot, then up the trail as they slogged through the mud and slush.

Daniel silently nodded in agreement.

The rain let up as they reached the tent where several deputy sheriffs milled around a folding table.

He and MD stood off to the side waiting to find out where they would be searching for victims.

Daniel checked his phone again, hoping Noah had left a message that he'd found Maggie, or at least a clue to where she was.

Nothing.

He shoved the phone back into his pocket. If he didn't hear back soon, he'd go look for her himself.

7

M aggie made it to what looked like a trail, but with all the debris strewn over the ground and snow quickly covering everything, she couldn't be sure. She stopped a moment to catch her breath and take a sip of water.

No one knew she'd come out here. She'd wanted to be alone, to grieve in private, and feel close to Colin on the anniversary of his death.

Well, you got what you wanted. You're totally alone.

"Not helpful," she said. Colin had never been one to mince words in life, or apparently in death.

Okay, so it hadn't been smart to come out here without telling anyone, but there was nothing she could do about that now. One good thing with the flooding, someone at Adventure Docs would be trying to reach her, and when they couldn't, a red flag would go up. But how soon that would be she didn't know, and she couldn't wait for a search party.

She started downhill, wishing yet again she had her walking sticks. The proverbial tortoise would be faster in comparison as the trail twisted and turned, making each step more slippery than the last.

Maggie rubbed her arms to dispel the cold. Her pants had dried, but her coat and the shirt underneath were still soggy and did little to combat the drop in temperature. If she couldn't make it to her car, she'd have to find shelter to survive the night.

Her feet dug into the mud as she started down a steep incline. The cold seeped into her bones and fatigue dogged her every step. Oh, what she wouldn't give to go back to those days with Daniel after their engagement. They'd both been so happy. Why couldn't they have stayed that way?

~

FIVE YEARS, five months ago...

The days dragged even with the constant flurry of activity at the aid station. Once Maggie admitted she was ready for home and hearth, she wanted nothing more than to be living in Paradise Falls, but she still had a month left before that happened and a wedding to plan.

She'd already applied for a life flight position at Paradise General. Colin continued to pester her to work at Adventure Docs, and while she was interested, it could be years before his dream came to fruition. She had to make a living in the meantime. If and when he and Daniel got Adventure Docs up and running, then she would consider working for them.

Maggie's phone beeped, a text from Daniel came across the screen. *Two weeks training in North Carolina. Three-day leave on the tenth. Fly in and join me?*

A long weekend with Daniel? A no brainer.

I'm all yours.

Time with Daniel was just what the doctor ordered.

~

MAGGIE CRACKED OPEN AN EYE, glaring at the early morning light that angled through the hotel window. A trail of clothing from the door to the bed littered the floor, her bra slung over the lampshade on the opposite side of the bed. How it got there she wasn't sure and didn't care. She'd arrived late last night, and there'd been no time for words. Every time they were together it was like a new beginning, and now that she'd made the decision to go home, she wanted more than the occasional weekend together.

The one thing she knew with certainty—she loved Daniel and wanted to marry him. The rest they would work out as they went along.

Daniel put his arm around her and snuggled her back against his chest. He left a row of kisses down her neck. She forgot about the future and focused on the present. A shudder swept over her like a frigid Idaho wind only instead of bracing against the cold, her breath caught in anticipation.

"You're certainly perky in the morning."

His raspy chuckle sent desire careening through her. "I like your play on words."

She arched her neck to allow him better access. "I thought you might." She fingered a lock of his hair.

His kisses moved across her shoulder and down her arm. Another shiver swept over her as he savored the tender flesh on the inside of her arm.

"I need sustenance," he said.

His lips brushed the side of her breast, eliciting a gasp from her.

"I don't need anything except more of what you're doing."

A rush of disappointment swept over her when his mouth moved away from her breast. He dipped his head and pressed a kiss to her lips. "Your wish is my command."

And just like the genie from the bottle, he made her every wish come true.

∾

MAGGIE CAME out of the shower the next morning to find Daniel dressed and packing. She'd hoped for one more romp before heading back to Poldivia. She came up to him and wrapped her arms around his waist.

He stiffened and she pulled back to look into his face. What she saw frightened her. "What's wrong?"

"Colin called while you were in the shower. Dad's had a heart attack."

Maggie's arms tightened around him. "He's alive?"

"Yes."

"What's his prognosis?"

His face stricken, he shook his head. "I don't know. All I know is he was out having breakfast and started having chest pains. He wasn't breathing when the ambulance arrived."

"When?" Maggie asked.

"About an hour ago."

Daniel dropped his head to her neck and drew in a ragged breath. He clung to her as if she were his salvation, the only thing that kept him functioning. "I can't lose him, Maggie. I just can't."

Her voice fierce, she said, "You won't. We'll make sure he's got the best care possible."

He lifted his head and gratitude shone in his eyes. "You're coming home with me?"

"Of course I am." Maggie tenderly brushed her fingers over his forehead. "Where else would I be when there's a family crisis?"

◇

MAGGIE SLEPT in snatches during the flight from North Carolina, dreaming of her childhood and specifically Tom Gregorio. Strong, dependable, but mostly Maggie remembered his laugh—warm and infectious. It was the kind of laugh that garnered attention, that drew a smile from the most stalwart and stern. Maggie held on to that memory when they arrived in Paradise Falls late that afternoon.

Daniel drove straight to the hospital. They found a semi-private corner in the waiting room and conferred with Tom's doctor.

"Your dad is a lucky man. Well, not total luck as he's in great shape, and that probably saved his life. I meant lucky because he got to the hospital so quickly. I expect he will have a complete recovery," Dr. Francis told them.

Daniel leaned forward, tension vibrating from him. "How long before he's back on his feet?"

"I can't give you an exact time frame, but your father is motivated, so it wouldn't surprise me if he was back to his normal routine in a few months."

Maggie clasped Daniel's hand and asked, "How much help will he need?"

"Quite a bit once he's released, then it should get better. My biggest concern is that he will try to push his recovery."

Daniel snorted. "My dad? Never."

Daniel's sarcasm produced a chuckle from the doctor, then his tone turned serious. "I only recall Dad being sick a few times growing up. He never stopped. He went to work, he took care of us, he just kept going."

Maggie gave his hand a reassuring squeeze. "He always seemed invincible, didn't he?"

Daniel offered her a weary smile. "He did."

A beat of silence passed before Maggie asked, "When will he be released?"

"If he continues as he has, I would say by the end of the week at the latest."

They discussed a few more details, then they went to see him.

Daniel gripped her hand as they entered the room. His barrel-chested brute of a father looked small and defenseless with tubes going in and out of his body. His eyes opened, and there was no mistaking relief when he saw them.

"You aren't AWOL, are you?" His attempt at humor drew an exasperated sigh from his son.

"No, Dad. I took an emergency leave."

Tom wagged a finger at her. "I see you brought my wayward girl home, too."

Maggie smiled and leaned forward to kiss his cheek. "I've missed you."

"Ditto that, kiddo," he whispered in her ear. "But you've been out doing good in the world."

"I've been trying." She gave him a stern look. "Have you been taking care of yourself?"

"Three meals a day like clockwork."

"A donut and coffee is not a meal."

Tom suppressed a smile. "Okay, two meals a day."

Maggie tucked in his blanket. "Well, we'll just see about that when we get you home. We'll have you in shipshape in no time."

Tom smiled and gave her a two finger salute. "Yes, ma'am."

Daniel slipped an arm around her waist. "We're here to help, Dad, and according to your doctor you may be coming home in a few days."

"When?"

"He said by the end of the week if everything keeps going as it is."

"Thank God. I'm sick to death of being poked and prodded."

Daniel moved to the side of the bed. "Colin's on his way home, too, and we'll be here as long as you need us."

Tom's brows drew together. "I'm not a three-year-old. I can take care of myself. You two have careers that you need to get back to."

Maggie squeezed Daniel's hand silently urging him to tread softly.

He gave her a barely perceptible nod. *Message received.*

"We're just going to pitch in until you can manage on your own—unless you'd rather we hire a nurse?" Daniel said.

Tom's scowl answered his question. "Strangers in my house would drive me to another heart attack." He gave them a dark look while he fought back a yawn. "The minute I'm well enough, you two and Colin are heading back. Got it?"

Daniel squeezed his shoulder. "Rest and we'll be back later."

"Okay." His words slurred as he drifted off to sleep.

They exited the hospital, and Maggie drove them to Tom's house. Once they were inside, she pressed Daniel into a chair at the kitchen table and fixed them both a sandwich, but they only picked at the food.

Daniel raked his fingers through his hair. "Jesus, he looked like hell. Tell me the doctor wasn't lying to us—that Dad's going to be okay."

Maggie scooted her chair closer and pressed her shoulder to his. "Yes, he looked weak, but considering he's recovering from a heart attack he looked good. Don't let all the what-ifs take over. Keep reminding yourself that he's strong, he's motivated, and he's in good hands."

He turned his face into her neck and murmured, "I can't lose my dad."

Maggie squeezed him tight and felt the same desperation. The thought of losing Tom was unthinkable. "I'm only telling you what you already know. Keep good thoughts for you and for him. It's what he needs most right now."

Daniel breathed in. "I'm so glad you're here. Dealing with all of this takes every ounce of energy I have."

Maggie rested her head on his shoulder. "You need sleep."

His gaze burned with a need that ignited a raging fire within her. "I need you." He kissed her with an intensity that sent urgent need rushing through her.

She didn't resist when he took her hand and led her upstairs to his room. The best comfort was losing themselves in each other.

～

PRESENT DAY...

Maggie's teeth chattered as she made her way down the mountain. She'd always admired Daniel's commitment to his family, and by extension she'd considered herself part of that family, until he shut her out and stopped talking to her.

Maggie concentrated on putting one foot in front of the other and worried about the present instead of the past. She didn't intend to die out here. She had plenty to live for, even if she didn't have Daniel.

8

D aniel and MD had just finished up with the sheriff's
department and search and rescue when Noah called him.
"We're at Maggie's house. Her SUV is gone and both
packs."

"The bigger one and the running pack?"

"Yes."

Concern blossomed. "No note?"

"Nothing."

"What about Lightning?"

"He's gone, too. What the hell is going on?"

Hell, hell, hell echoed in the background as baby Jon singsonged
his dad's words.

Daniel didn't want to voice his fears aloud, but if the apprehension curling in his gut was any indication, he'd need every hand on
deck. "I'm at Pine Ridge. We were called in to assist with a flash flood.
We've been trying to contact Maggie for the past hour and her cell
goes straight to voicemail."

Silence other than Jon chanting *hell, hell, hell.*

"She always has her phone with her since that time she got
injured when she was out running," Daniel said.

"I'm on my way back to the house to leave Jon with Abby and grab my gear. Then I'll start checking her favorite trails."

"Keep me posted. I'm calling Liam. He said he could get away to help search," Daniel said. "Get as many people as you can."

Silence fell between them and the fear gnawing at Daniel intensified when he sensed Noah felt it, too.

"I'll start making calls," Noah said at last.

Daniel ended the call. A chill swept over him the same as the time he'd come home and only Lightning had been waiting for him.

~

Five years ago...

A bomb ignited. The vehicle in front of Daniel lifted off the ground and skidded across the sand. Gunfire erupted. They slammed into the ditch. The Kid opened the door, but Daniel yanked him back.

Gunfire pinged off the metal-sided vehicle.

"Incoming."

Daniel sucked in a breath, his eyes snapping open. His heart thundered in his chest as he waited for the nightmare to subside.

He burrowed deeper under the covers and watched Maggie sleep. Just watching her peaceful slumber soothed him. He resisted the urge to brush his fingers across her cheek. Instead, he slipped out of bed, the nightmare fading as he turned up the heat in the tiny apartment. The heater rumbled to life with a burst of cold air, followed a few minutes later with by warm air. When he and Maggie got their own place, they'd have a wood stove.

He tiptoed back to the bedroom, grabbed his clothes, and dressed in the bathroom to keep from waking Maggie. She'd worked overtime at the hospital last night when another nurse called in sick, so he imagined she'd sleep most of the morning away.

Not a morning person anyway, the night shift was ideal for her.

A wave of envy swept over him. He used to sleep like that, but not since they lost The Kid. Neither the team's effort nor Daniel's medical skills had been enough to save the fresh-faced farm boy.

They'd lost The Kid on Daniel's last mission. And in the four months since they'd buried him, he'd retired from the military and come home to build a life with Maggie. But the nightmare stayed with him.

He shook off the memory. He couldn't focus on the past or it would eat him alive. He grabbed his jacket and headed to his dad's for breakfast—a weekly date since his dad's heart attack six months ago.

Daniel had received a humanitarian reassignment while his dad recuperated, then he'd gone back to finish his commitment. During that same time, Maggie completed her obligation with World Health Center.

They'd returned home in May and rented this tiny apartment while they searched for a home to buy. But between Maggie's crazy work schedule and getting Adventure Docs up and running, they still hadn't found a house. But that would change, and soon.

Lightning, their six-month-old Lab puppy, needed a yard. Besides, they were both ready to settle down with a home of their own. Him, more so than Maggie. He'd had enough of the nomadic life. He wanted stability and to start a family of his own. He wanted what Maggie had grown up with—lots and lots of family. It had only been his dad, Colin, and him after their mom died.

Daniel still remembered the accident as if it happened yesterday. He'd been five and riding in the back seat entertaining Colin on the way home from school. A truck had come through the intersection and hit them. As his mom lay bleeding, she made him promise to watch over his brother. At the time, he'd taken it to mean forever. As an adult, he realized she'd meant until help arrived. But even so, he protected Colin and always would.

Daniel scribbled Maggie a note, telling her he'd be home by three, then drove to his dad's. He went straight to the kitchen and poured himself a cup of coffee. He inhaled and savored the rich aroma.

His dad's gruff voice echoed from the other side of the kitchen where he took plates from the cupboard. "Where's our girl? I thought she'd come, too."

Daniel added cream to his coffee. "She worked a double shift, so she's still sleeping."

"Give her a kiss for me when you get home."

Daniel smiled. His dad was as in love with Maggie as he was.

He set an omelet in front of him. "How's Adventure Docs coming along?"

Daniel exhaled a weary breath. "Taking a lot more time than I anticipated." He wanted more time with Maggie, but at the same time keeping busy helped him forget the nightmares.

His dad made a sympathetic grunt as he grabbed a bagel from the toaster. "When I started my plumbing business, it seemed like I spent more time at the bank and with the accountants than actually working."

"That's exactly how it's feeling. I wish Colin were here to handle this part. If I didn't know better, I'd think he stayed away just to stick me with it."

His dad topped off his coffee, then sat down across from him, chuckling. "You know, I wouldn't put it past your brother to do that. He always was pretty sly that way, but I doubt even he could pull this off."

Daniel had to agree. "So, are you enjoying retirement?"

A light sparked in his dad's eyes. "Every damn minute of it. Golfing, fishing, hiking whenever I feel like it. Wish it hadn't taken a heart attack to drive me to it."

"But if you hadn't had it, you'd still be working and missing out on all the things retirement has to offer."

His dad held up his coffee mug. "To retirement."

Daniel clinked his cup and wished his dad many, many years filled with good health. He scarfed down his omelet and piled more hash browns onto his plate.

"There's plenty more in the kitchen."

"This will do me. Thanks, Dad." He took a bite and the potatoes were done to perfection. His father was a damn good cook, and the reason he and Colin had never lacked for a meal growing up. "Have you spoken to Colin lately?"

"Only by email a few days ago."

"Did he say if his tour was finishing up on schedule?"

His dad cradled his coffee mug between his hands and studied him. "Is the paperwork really that bad?"

Daniel grunted. The paperwork sucked, but he was managing it. "No, it's not that bad. I was just curious is all." Still he hoped nothing delayed his brother's return because he was banking on having him here when they opened. Adventure Docs had been his brainchild after all, and it was only fitting that he be here for the grand opening.

They talked as Daniel finished eating, then he carried his dishes to the kitchen and started cleaning up.

"Leave it," his dad ordered. "I'm retired. I'll handle it. You've got things to do."

He did, but he didn't like dumping the clean up on his dad, especially after he'd made him breakfast.

He shoved a thermos of coffee at him. "For the road, now go do something productive with your day and leave an old retired guy to his loafing."

Daniel took the coffee, then headed out to his car. Anxiety wove through him. What would he have done if his dad hadn't survived that heart attack?

~

DANIEL ARRIVED at Georgia's Diner at noon to meet MD and Sloan. They had both decided not to reenlist, and since both were rabid outdoor enthusiasts, Daniel had contacted them to see if they would consider becoming part of Adventure Docs.

The three of them sat at a scarred picnic table that overlooked the Serenity River.

MD took a swig of his beer. "So, what's this plan of yours?"

Daniel took a moment to collect his thoughts before responding. "Not mine, Colin's."

Sloan snorted and choked on the beer he'd just swallowed. "Colin! God help us. What exactly are you dragging us into?"

Daniel had had the same reaction when Colin proposed the idea to him. He wasn't sure if he'd be diving out of an airplane naked or hanging upside down on a rock wall, and frankly he still wasn't sure that wouldn't happen given his brother's penchant for living life on the edge. Not that Daniel didn't like to live life balls to the wall, but his brother took adventure to the *extreme*—a place Daniel had never gone and never would. He'd had enough of that in the military.

"Colin came up with the idea of Adventure Docs. We will provide medical backup for sporting events and position ourselves to be where medical services are needed. Say, if it's a triathlon, one of us would be on the water in a kayak. Or if it's a surfing competition, we'd be out on a board or a jet ski. There will be lots of traveling, too. The way I see it, we can combine work with the sports we love to do. We'd also provide training for the military, fire departments, and search and rescue."

Sloan munched on a French fry. "Mountain biking, motocross, marathons."

"Concerts and festivals, too," MD interjected.

"Exactly. Colin thinks we should promote our military experience, our medical training, our conditioning," Daniel said.

Sloan swirled another fry through the ketchup on his plate. "This is going to require some heavy duty financing to really do it right."

"The financing is covered." He and Colin were splitting it fifty/fifty. Colin had earned enough playing baseball to cover his and Daniel had been stashing money away, but he'd had to take out a loan, too.

Silence as they contemplated his offer.

Daniel held up his hand. "Hey, no hard feelings if you're not interested. It's a startup business and it's risky. I can't promise you a job a year from now."

MD glared at him. "What the hell? You tempt us with this, and then try to talk us out of it. You aren't much of a salesman, Gregorio."

Sloan's laughter rumbled across the patio. "What MD said. And for the record, I'm a self-proclaimed adrenaline junkie, and my high is taking risks. This sounds like a perfect fit for me. Count me in."

"Me, too," MD said. "What's the next step?"

"I already have three trainings lined up to cover as soon as we open. And Colin has been working on procuring some military training gigs, plus he's lined up work with the Forest Service covering fires, but we won't open for a couple of months still, which gives you two time to get your EMT training done."

MD scowled. "You want us to go back to fucking school."

"Suck it up, asshole. Of course he does. Kind of hard to be part of *Adventure Docs* without some kind of medical training." Sloan looked at Daniel. "So what will you be doing while we suffer through these classes?"

Daniel held up the list of things he had to accomplish before the grand opening.

"Jesus, Colin's got you doing his bidding like you're his private lap dog, doesn't he?" MD said.

Daniel frowned. "I'm not his lackey."

MD snickered. "Could have fooled me."

In truth, Daniel was starting to feel like his brother's minion even though he knew Colin would be doing his part if he were stateside. But he sure as hell wasn't telling them that. He held up his bottle.

"It's time to christen our new venture. To Adventure Docs."

Sloan and MD held up their beers. "To Adventure Docs."

～

DANIEL FINISHED up early and headed home, eager to see Maggie. He'd been worried that when they'd come home for good that it might be an adjustment being together all the time, but he'd found it was just the opposite. The more time he spent with her, the more he wanted to be with her. So, when only Lightning greeted him, he was disappointed.

He called her cell, and it rang in their bedroom. He followed the sound to her nightstand, right where she'd left it—again.

He searched for a note and found nothing. He checked the

carport in back and found her car parked in the usual spot. She must have gone for a run, but for how long and where?

Something felt off, but he couldn't put his finger on exactly what, but everything left him anxious lately—so much so he didn't trust his instincts.

He checked the time.

Four-thirty.

Lightning whined.

Daniel took him outside, but instead of relieving himself, he tugged on the leash, dragging him to the trail adjacent to the apartment complex. "No, we're going to stay here and wait for Maggie to come home."

He led him back to the grass, but Lightning turned and stared at the trail, releasing a long, low whine.

Daniel watched the afternoon sun start its descent. Why wasn't Maggie home?

He studied the surrounding area, but saw no sign of her.

Sunset was less than an hour away. And with the darkness came the cold and temps were predicted in the thirties—even lower in the higher elevations tonight.

Lightning barked and yanked on the leash. "Okay, boy, let's go get my gear."

Daniel changed into warm clothes, then grabbed his backpack loaded with medical supplies, food, and a sleeping bag. He took the trail, giving Lightning the lead. The dog took him straight to Devil's Peak. Tension snaked through him when he found Maggie's bike chained to a post at the trailhead. At least they were on the right track.

Daniel dug out his headlamp and slipped it on, then unclipped the leash. "Find her, boy."

Lightning shot up a sharp incline and Daniel followed, calling out Maggie's name.

No response, just the echo of his own voice.

He shouted again. "Maggie!"

He stopped to catch his breath and listen for a response.

Silence, other than Lightning's panting.

Daniel signaled the dog and started running again, but he had to slow his pace because of the uneven terrain from the recent rains that had left deep ruts in the trail.

Who in their right mind would run this?

Colin for sure, and Maggie, too. The more challenging the trail, the more likely they were to try it, except Maggie generally had more sense than his brother.

"Maggie."

His shout set off a pack of coyotes. Their frenzied response started a low rumbling in Lightning's chest. Daniel envisioned Maggie hurt and unable to defend herself. He picked up his pace. He had to find her before something else did.

The trail twisted and curved, making a steep climb that had him winded by the time he reached the rise. The sun dipped over the horizon, and he started running again, calling out her name.

He was already three miles in, and knowing Maggie she could have planned a ten-mile run or more.

He'd covered another two miles when full darkness settled over him.

"Maggie."

No response.

He rounded a bend and in the distance he just made out the shadowy image of a cabin, smoke curling from the chimney.

Lightning raced forward, pawed at the door, then whined. Daniel burst into the cabin, his pulse thumping in his throat and the perspiration drenching him from more than just his body's exertion.

He went weak with relief when he found Maggie huddled over a fire in the old wood stove, alive and well, then fury shook him.

"Daniel!"

He grabbed her and pulled her close, the anger pulsing through him making him want to shake her. Instead, he eased his hold and contained his anger. "Are you okay? Are you hurt?"

She released a snort of disgust. "I'm fine. The only thing smarting more than my pride is my pulled hamstring."

"How bad is it?"

She eased back down onto the log she'd used as a chair. Lightning sat beside her, dropping his head on her shoulder and watching her intently. "Bad enough that I'd kill for some Ibuprofen right now."

Daniel slipped off his pack, took out the first aid kit, and handed her a couple of pills and a bottle of water.

She swallowed them while he rummaged in his pack for an elastic bandage.

"You're such a Boy Scout." Pain interlaced her teasing tone.

He held two fingers to his forehead. "Our motto is always be prepared, ma'am."

Her teeth flashed white in the dim room lit only by the fire. "I see why you went into medicine."

He'd done it because of his mom. Being prepared hadn't topped the list. It was just an added benefit. "I chose medicine because I like helping people."

She leaned in close. "Something else you're very good at," she murmured against his lips.

Daniel pressed his palm to the back of her head and deepened the kiss, his pent up emotions spilling out.

Lightning wedged himself between them and barked.

Daniel pulled back, laughing, and handed him a biscuit. He gobbled it up in one bite and begged for another. He gave him a second one and some water, then continued his search for the bandage.

"How did you find me?"

"Dumb luck."

She shook her head. "You don't believe in luck. You always have a plan."

He found the bandage and held it up. "True, but this time I had Lightning. He led me to you."

"Good boy." Maggie hugged the pup and wrinkled her nose when she received a wet, sloppy kiss across her face.

Daniel slid the bandage up her calf and secured it to her thigh.

"This should make it easier for you to walk when we start home in the morning."

"I should have been smart enough to bring my own first aid kit."

"It would only slow you down."

"You brought one."

He rummaged through the pack. "I wasn't running for speed. I brought it because I was afraid you might—" He stopped and swallowed past the knot of fear lodged in his throat. "—I was afraid you might be hurt."

Maggie pressed her fingers to his cheek. "And you were right."

"But if I were headed out to run I wouldn't have brought it." His comment brought a smile to her lips that faded with his next words. "But you didn't use your head. A phone weighs almost nothing." He gestured to Lightning. "He weighs nothing at all, and he needs exercise."

Her eyebrows drew together. "I'm not a child, Daniel, and I don't appreciate being treated like one."

His anger flashed again. "Then don't behave like one." He sucked in a deep breath and controlled it. "Do you have any idea how awful it is to come home and find you gone? No note—nothing—not a clue where you'd gone. I'm not asking for a blow-by-blow of your every movement. I'm just asking that you leave me a note when you're going for a run and to take your phone." He controlled the tremor in his voice with an effort. "I love you, Maggie, and the idea of losing you out here scares the hell out of me."

Silence followed his outburst.

"I'm sorry. I didn't think. I'm not used to answering to anyone."

He tenderly tucked a lock of hair behind her ear. "I know. We've been apart more than we've been together, so it's going to take some getting used to." He hesitated a moment then said, "But please don't go off like that again without letting me know where you're headed. I'd die if something happened to you."

She brushed the hair from his forehead. "I swear I'll always be there for you. You didn't happen to bring anything to eat did you?"

He arched a brow at her. "How long have I known you?"

"Hopefully long enough to know I'd want food on my deathbed."

He handed her a nutrition bar. "Start with this, then I'll make you something more substantial."

She tore open the wrapper and devoured it, while he spread out the sleeping bag on the floor.

"How far did you run?"

"Ten miles. I was hoping to make a fifteen-mile loop. Damn it, this injury is going to set me back for a while."

"I'm afraid it will."

"Do you have any more of those bars?"

He handed her another one. She started to open it, then looked up at him. "Thank you for coming."

He swiped a loose strand of hair from her face. "You knew I'd come looking."

"I did, but just because I expected it doesn't mean I'm not grateful." Her belly rumbled again.

He eased her onto the sleeping bag. "Eat and rest while I make us some dinner."

She opened the bar and began eating. "That wasn't Ibuprofen, was it?"

"No, it was a little stronger."

"It's working." Her voice drifted as she laid down. "Wake me up when dinner's ready if I doze off."

He took a blanket from his pack and unfolded it, laying it over her. She smiled and took his hand, kissing his palm. "Thank you. I will make this up to you later."

She drifted off to sleep, and his heart thudded in his chest. What would he have done if something had happened to her?

Life without Maggie? Inconceivable.

The very idea sent him into a cold sweat. She made him whole, made life worth living.

He put more wood on the fire, then took a fistful of MREs from his pack. Not great, but better than nothing.

He found a pan in the tiny kitchen, filled it water and set it on the woodstove to heat. While he waited for it to boil, he sat down beside Maggie watching the firelight play on her face.

While he'd never wish an injury on her, he was grateful for some time alone with her. Ever since their return to Paradise Falls they'd had little time together between Maggie's hours at the hospital and all the time he'd put in to get Adventure Docs rolling.

The water boiled and he made coffee. The scent of it brought Maggie around. He opened packages of pepper steak, added the water, then handed one to her.

Her voice still slurred with sleep, she said, "A romantic dinner for two."

He handed her a plastic fork. "It's not the greatest meal I've ever cooked, but it will fill you up."

She smiled at him. "It's perfect. Thank you."

He found two mugs and filled them with coffee, handing her one.

She inhaled the strong brew. "Fabulous," she murmured, then sipped it and scowled. "That will put hair on your chest."

He tossed her a packet of sugar. "This should help."

She dumped it in and stirred it with her fork, then sipped.

"Better?" he asked.

"Much."

He scooted next to her, sipping his coffee.

"You're tough to drink that without sugar."

"I can take more hair on my chest—you can't."

She laughed. "It would look better on you." She tasted her food. "Delicious."

"I wouldn't go that far."

"I would. When you're starving, you don't care what you eat."

There was a lot of truth to that.

They finished their meals, and Daniel opened apple pies for dessert. When they were finished, Maggie patted her belly. "Much better. What did you bring for breakfast?"

Daniel burst out laughing. "It's a surprise. You'll have to wait to find out. I'll even serve you breakfast in bed."

Her lower lip jutted. "You know I hate surprises."

She reached for his backpack, but he nudged it aside with his toe. "I won't be able to sleep without knowing."

"I'll find a way to keep your mind occupied with other things."

Her eyes twinkled, desire lighting the blue depths. "Like what?"

He whispered a suggestion in her ear. "If you're up to it, that is."

"With the painkillers you gave me, I'm up for anything."

He added more wood to the fire, opened the sleeping bag, and set about putting his suggestion into motion.

◞

ONLY A FEW EMBERS remained in the fire when he awoke the next morning. He stoked it, and within minutes the fire was roaring again.

Maggie stretched and opened her eyes, humor sparkling in their depths. "So, where is my breakfast in bed?"

Daniel set a pan filled with water on the woodstove for their coffee. "You are a very impatient woman, Maggie Murphy."

"I can be."

There was clearly more than food on her mind.

"Is the coffee going to be a while?"

"A few minutes for sure."

She crooked a finger at him. "Then why don't you come over here and warm me up?"

Not one to ignore a lady's request, he did her bidding again and again and again. Much later he fed her breakfast in bed as promised, but in an entirely different way than she expected.

◞

PRESENT DAY...

From that day on, Maggie always took Lightning and her phone, and left a note telling Daniel where she was headed—until the day she left him. There had been no note, just an empty closet that required no explanation. She'd left because of him, and until he controlled his anger, he didn't want her anywhere near him.

He and MD lugged the gear to the triage station they'd set up for potential victims.

MD pounded a tent stake into the muddy ground. "Maggie is fine. She can take care of herself. She's got more grit than any man or woman I know." He jabbed Daniel in the side. "Hell, she put up with you until you became a total ass."

Daniel grimaced. "Yeah, I'm an ass."

"You are. What the hell is wrong with you?"

Daniel hadn't confided in anyone the real reason for their breakup—his bursts of anger, his silence and the nightmares, but mostly his inability to let go of his guilt, had sent Maggie packing. That had ended their marriage with more finality than shutting the lid on Colin's casket.

MD's voice intruded into his thoughts. "So, what are you going to do to get her back?"

Daniel stared at his friend wishing he could do just that, but the truth was he was terrified that one day he'd snap like other soldiers he knew and hurt Maggie with more than harsh words.

9

M aggie pushed her way through a thick maze of brush. Her forward motion came to an abrupt end at a wall of rock covered in a fresh layer of snow. Shivers wracked her body as she searched for an alternate route.

Options: scale the rock wall or backtrack since there was no way around it.

Retracing her steps wasn't appealing, but it beat slipping and falling to her death.

Another shiver set her teeth to chattering.

Move now or die, Mags.

Colin's image wavered through the falling snow.

"I'm tired. I can't do this anymore."

The hell you can't. MOVE.

The image vanished.

Colin had always known just what to say to get her motivated.

She started back the way she'd come. Two steps forward and one back to finding her way down the mountain. The same as her relationship with Daniel or so it seemed.

He was everything she'd ever wanted in a man. Kind, considerate, courageous. He'd supported her desire for a small wedding against strong pressure from her family, even though he'd wanted the big wedding with all the frills.

∽

FOUR YEARS, *six months ago...*

Maggie did everything possible to avoid the last-minute wedding preparations. She'd given her mother and sister, Becky, permission to do as they saw fit, but at the same time her stomach was coiled in knots. All she wanted was a small, intimate wedding without all the frou-frou, but her mother, in particular, loved to decorate, and if she hadn't become a nutritionist, Maggie was certain she'd have been a party planner.

She watched Daniel as he prepared breakfast for them and chatted about the wedding details. Was there something wrong with her? Why was he more into their nuptials than she was?

"I'm picking up the tuxes on Friday afternoon."

Maggie finished setting the table and faced Daniel. "Is something wrong with me?"

His hands stilled, the pancake batter momentarily forgotten as he focused on her, giving her a slow onceover. "Something wrong with you how?"

"I'm not talking about my body, you goof, I meant the wedding. I would have been perfectly happy just going to city hall and having Judge Tompkins do the ceremony."

His smile melted her through and through. He stepped around the counter and tenderly kissed her. "There is nothing wrong with you." He tapped the end of her nose. "In fact, I find your disinterest one of your more endearing qualities."

He always knew exactly what to say to make her feel special. "I have more than one?"

He grinned. "You most definitely do." He stepped back to the stove and expertly flipped the pancakes.

"I want to hear more about them."

He checked the underside of the pancakes, then slid them onto a plate before shooting her a wink over his shoulder. "Well, there's so many it may take me a while to list them all."

Maggie settled back in her chair. "I've got nowhere else to be. Start talking, loverboy."

He set a platter of fluffy pancakes and bacon in front of her, and she momentarily forgot what they'd been discussing until he sat down beside her and began listing off all of the qualities he loved about her.

"You're kind, thoughtful, generous—you appreciate my cooking." He wiggled his eyebrows, and she smiled around a mouthful of pancake.

He leaned in and pressed a kiss to the tender spot behind her ear. "I especially love a woman with a healthy appetite."

The purr of his voice sent a tingle of awareness down her spine that intimated he referred to more than food. "What exactly are you implying?"

"I'm saying, hurry up and finish your breakfast, so we can take care of some other appetites."

She dipped another bite of pancake into the syrup and shot him a sassy grin. "You know how I like to savor my food."

His eyes warmed with appreciation. "Another trait I love about you—the fact that you savor everything."

Suddenly she no longer wanted pancakes—she wanted him. She shoved away from the table, picked up the last piece of bacon from her plate and waved it at him.

"I've decided to take my breakfast to go. Care to join me?"

His eyes danced with merriment and the promise of a trip to heaven and back. "Are you going to share or make me starve?"

She wiggled her hips. "I'm always willing to share."

Daniel made a lunge for her, but she sidestepped him and ran for the bedroom, her laughter trailing after her. "You're going to have to do better than that."

He swooped her into his arms just before she crossed the threshold. "Let me show you what I can do."

She sighed, her concerns about the wedding forgotten, which she suspected had been his intent all along. She wrapped her arms around his neck and pressed a kiss to the pulse beating at the base of his neck and experienced a thrill when it pumped harder.

It didn't matter that she wasn't a woman interested in all the girly stuff. What mattered was she was the kind of woman Daniel loved.

∼

MAGGIE AND DANIEL drove to the airport to pick up Colin two days before the wedding, leaving the last-minute details of the wedding in her mother and sister's capable hands. Maggie sensed they were relieved to have her gone so that they didn't have to keep deferring to her and getting I-don't-knows and I-don't-cares for their effort.

Instead of stressing over something that meant more to her mother and sister than it did to her, she focused on enjoying the ride to Spokane, a relaxing lunch, and seeing Colin. She hadn't spoken to him in two weeks and was anxious to see him in person.

"I'm still surprised Tom didn't want to come with us," Maggie said.

"Me, too, but Dad said he'd promised your mom he'd do something for the wedding."

"Like what?"

"No idea, but it had to be important to keep him from coming with us."

A shiver of apprehension crawled up Maggie's spine. "Knowing Mom, it's probably a giant waterfall or something equally over the top."

Daniel let off the gas. "It's not too late to stay and help them decorate."

Maggie seriously contemplated the suggestion, then blew out a breath. "No, I told them to do what they wanted—that I'd trust them to make it look nice."

Daniel squeezed her hand. "Then relax and enjoy the day."

Easy for him to say, but she took his advice and pushed aside her concerns.

They arrived at the airport by ten and still had to wait an hour for Colin's plane to arrive.

When Colin came down the escalator the media swarmed him, stopping him in his tracks. He'd left baseball almost two years ago, and he was more popular now than when he'd been playing. Baseball star turned decorated soldier made for the perfect hero.

Maggie jumped up and down waving, her heart pumping with excitement even though he couldn't see her through the mass of people. She didn't care. Colin was home, but her joy faded when she saw his face. Something was different—wrong.

She watched as Colin answered the media questions with the same patience and affability that had won the hearts of the press and baseball fans everywhere, but behind his cordial expression lurked suffering.

She'd heard it in his voice last time they talked, but now, seeing his face as he said goodbye to the reporters and headed over to them, she could tell something was definitely wrong.

Before she could comment, he swooped her into his arms and swung her around, then set her on the polished floor. "It's so good to be home."

He released her and turned to hug his brother. "How's the business coming along?"

Daniel grinned, but Maggie saw the same uneasiness in his expression. "I'm making progress. I'll be damned glad when you finish this tour and come home permanently to carry your share of the work."

Daniel picked up Colin's bag and ushered them both toward the parking lot. "Come on. We've got a wedding to attend, and Maggie skipped out on the decorating. She's worried Dad's helping her mom and Becky turn it into a Kardashian affair."

Maggie shuddered, then shook a finger at Daniel. "That isn't funny, and if that happens, we're eloping."

Daniel merely smiled in response. "You're the one who said all you wanted was an outdoor wedding, and then you turned it over to your mom and sister to make it happen. If you don't like the outcome, you've got no one to blame but yourself."

She wrinkled her nose. "What kind of groom throws a bride's words back in her face two days before the wedding?"

Colin answered before Daniel could respond. "A smart one, that's who."

Maggie punched Colin's shoulder. "I thought you were my friend, and here you are ganging up on me with your brother. Some pal you are."

Colin held up a hand and shot a conspiratorial wink at Daniel. "Hey, you know I'm always there for you, but this is one of those bro-backing-bro instances."

Maggie stopped walking, put her hands on her hips, and glared at the two. "Oh that's lame. You're just taking the easy way out."

Colin wrapped an arm around her shoulder and urged her forward. "I can't always side with you."

Maggie snorted, but was appeased. Here was the Colin she knew and loved, but still she sensed something was off with him. She just couldn't put her finger on what, but she would find out.

~

MAGGIE HAD PLANNED on checking out the wedding site after the rehearsal dinner, then sleeping in her own bed the night before the wedding, but her sister and the rest of the wedding party swooped her off to a little bed and breakfast for one last "girl's night" as Becky called it.

The night included facials, manicures and pedicures, and massages. The first three she tolerated, but the last was divine. She'd take the massage any day.

Immediately after breakfast the next morning, Becky dragged her downstairs where a beautician waited to do her hair. She blew out a weighted sigh and decided getting her hair done was easier to tolerate than all the jittery females upstairs. And she only had to get through today, then she and Daniel would be off on their honeymoon in Canada. That made it all worthwhile.

After considerable negotiations with the hairdresser, she managed to keep the style simple and elegant, rather than the mass of riotous curls her sister insisted on.

They arrived at Noah's lakefront home on Lake Serenity a little before two.

She tried to peek at the decorations, but Becky and her mother ushered her inside to dress before she could.

"You'll have plenty of time to take it all in after the ceremony," Becky assured her.

An hour later, her father waited for her at the bedroom door. "Ready, champion?"

Her dad's voice melted away her attack of nerves, and she relaxed. His reassuring presence eased the strain between her shoulders and she smiled up at him.

"I've never been more ready for anything in my life."

She placed her hand in the crook of his arm, and he pressed a kiss to the top of her head. "I know I had my reservations, but you made a good choice."

They followed the carpet laid on the ground to protect her gown.

The "Wedding March" began, and Becky nudged her. "Show time."

The swarm of butterflies returned, and she prayed she wouldn't be sick when she saw the entire yard filled to brimming with friends and family—all eyes focused on her.

This was a small wedding?

≈

PAPER LAMPS GLOWED across her brother's deck as Colin swung Maggie around the dance floor.

I've got this feeling. I've got to dance, dance, dance.

Colin spun her again and her laughter echoed above the music.

C'mon c'mon, let's dance, dance, dance.

At least they'd reached the part of the wedding celebration she actually enjoyed. The song ended, and Colin twirled her one last time over to Daniel sitting on the sidelines sipping a beer.

Maggie came to rest on his knee, laughter bubbling from her again as she fell against his chest. His arm slid around her waist and held her in place. His eyes deepened, and her heart beat a little faster. This was the man she'd married, the man she'd loved for as long as she could remember.

"Aw c'mon. Get a room."

Maggie leaned toward Colin who'd taken the chair next to Daniel and yelled in his ear to be heard above the music. "I put up with the wedding, so you have to put up with a few snuggles and kisses."

Colin scowled at her. "Okay, but just today. I don't want to see any of this stuff at Adventure Docs."

A devious grin crossed Daniel's lips. "Good luck with that."

They all laughed, but Maggie didn't miss the haunted look in Colin's eyes. Before she could ask, Daniel whisked her onto the dance floor, and she forgot about everything but him.

∿

Present day...

Not only had Maggie sensed something was wrong with Colin when he'd come home for their wedding, but later when she and Daniel looked at the wedding photos, she saw it in the smile that didn't quite reach his eyes, the haunted look in his expression. She'd known something was wrong, that he was upset and distant, but she'd been too preoccupied with the wedding to press him for answers. If she had, he might have opened up and told her what had happened in Afghanistan, then she could have helped him.

Of course she could say the same with Daniel. When his outbursts of anger became more frequent, she'd tried to reason with him, but he'd refused to talk to her. If only she hadn't given up and walked away from their marriage, maybe she could have reached him.

Maggie pushed aside the past and focused on putting one foot in front of the other. She stumbled and caught herself, but not before pain shot up the back of her thigh toppling her to the ground. She groaned, massaging her hamstring and finally easing the pain.

Struggling to her feet, she found a stick to help her get moving the same as she'd done after she filed for divorce. Daniel had signed the papers without protest and gotten on with his life.

Why couldn't she do the same?

10

Daniel studied the snow falling from fat storm clouds as he talked to Sloan on his cell phone. "Any word on Maggie?"

"Nothing. Still going to voicemail. Her SUV is gone. Noah and Liam have split up, and they're checking her favorite trails," Sloan said.

Shit, that meant they'd have to widen their search because she had a laundry list of places she ran regularly. "Is there any chance of tracking her phone?"

"I'm looking into it."

"Keep me posted." Daniel tucked the phone back into his pocket and zipped it closed.

"Any sign of her?" MD asked as he came out of the van with a pair of backpacks.

"Nothing. Sloan's going to try and track her phone."

"If anyone can do that, it's Pretty Boy."

MD tossed a pack at him and they set off to search for victims. Waiting and twiddling their thumbs wasn't their style and never had been. Adventure Docs did just like the name implied—adventure, but in this instance, they actively searched for victims with Maggie at the top of the list. It was how Colin intended for them to operate and what made them unique—what had made his brother special.

The muddy, wet ground made for treacherous walking and impeded their progress.

The bushes rustled behind them. Daniel turned in time to see a flash of white charge toward them.

MD's boot caught on an exposed root as Lightning flew past him heading straight for Daniel. He plowed into Daniel, knocking him to the ground, immediately licking his face.

Laughing, Daniel hugged him close, then pulled back. "What happened to you, boy? You're covered in mud." Daniel looked at MD. "You know what Lightning's being here means, don't you?"

MD's grim expression, matched the anxiety clutching at Daniel's heart. "Yeah. Mags is out here somewhere, and if the mud caked on his coat is any indication, they were caught in the flash flood."

"We've got to get moving."

MD nodded, then groaned when he tried to stand.

"Are you hurt?"

"Twisted my ankle on that damn root."

MD gingerly removed his boot and sock. The ankle was already puffy and swollen, but whether he'd bruised or fractured it, Daniel couldn't tell.

"Well, what do you think?"

"It looks like you're done for the day."

"Damn it."

Daniel helped him to his feet and slung an arm under his shoulder. "Let's get you to the hospital and get this x-rayed."

"I'll be fine. Just get me to the van, and I'll ice it while you get back out there and look for Maggie."

Daniel desperately wanted to do just that, but he couldn't just leave his friend and partner alone and injured. "We need to get you to the hospital and get this checked out."

"It'll wait until we're done out here."

Daniel was torn. MD needed to have this looked at, but Maggie was out there—he knew it with every fiber of his being.

MD grabbed his arm. "People could die—Maggie could die because you wasted time over what is most likely a sprain."

Daniel hesitated, and MD took advantage of his indecision.

"You don't want that on your conscience and neither do I, so just get me to the damn van."

Daniel couldn't deny the truth of his words, and if the situation were reversed, he'd do the same. So, he hauled MD to the van, got him settled, then picked up his pack and he and Lightning set off, leaving MD to notify the others that they'd found Lightning.

"Go find Maggie," he told the dog.

Lightning started up the trail then veered right. Daniel followed, scaling fallen trees and downed brush. His boots slid on the mud-slick ground. He skidded and went down. Lightning was immediately at his side.

He started to push to his feet, then froze when the hackles rose on Lightning's back and a growl rumbled in his chest.

Daniel looked up to find himself face-to-face with a very angry moose. All the times he'd cautioned Maggie to be careful in the wilderness, he was the one in danger this time.

~

Four years ago...

Daniel went from one appointment to the next, grabbed lunch on his way to a potential office site for Adventure Docs, scarfing down the sandwich as he drove. He thought leaving the military would give him more time with Maggie, but they barely saw each other. Once the business opened, he would make time for a life.

Sloan and MD agreed to meet him at the site after their EMT classes at the community college were done for the day.

They walked to the rear of the property where the shop was located and MD yawned.

"We keeping you up?" Daniel teased.

"As a matter-of-fact, you are. This classwork is kicking my ass. I'll take our training days back in the Corps any day."

Sloan agreed. "Sitting at a desk is brutal. I'd much rather do a ten-mile run."

Daniel unlocked the shop door. "All the more reason to check this place out so we can get Adventure Docs off the ground."

MD sucked down a long swallow of his energy drink. "Okay, I'm through whining. Let's get this done."

He and Sloan followed him inside.

Sloan whistled. "Nice space. This should give us plenty of room."

Daniel agreed. It was large enough for two vans, and there was plenty of storage area, too. He snapped several pictures to send to Colin, Sloan and MD hamming it up in the background.

They left the shop and walked to the house that would serve as their office. The back door opened into a small kitchen/dining room that led to a living room and bathroom with a full bedroom.

"We could use the living room as a command center," MD said.

Daniel agreed.

They went down to the fully finished basement, converted into a gym with the latest equipment.

MD stroked the weight machine like he would a woman. "Holy shit. I'm getting hard just looking at this."

Sloan snorted out a laugh. "Everything gives you a hard-on."

"Not everything, but damn close."

His comment drew a laugh from Daniel and Sloan.

"What are the chances this equipment comes with the place?" Sloan asked.

Daniel checked out the rowing machine. "If I were selling it, I sure as hell wouldn't want to lug all this stuff up those stairs."

"Me, either. Make the owners an offer they can't refuse," MD advised.

Daniel took more pictures of the basement and house, then sent them all to Colin. "I just hope Colin's on board."

"Fuck Colin. He's not here. Make an executive decision," MD said.

Daniel chuckled and didn't disagree, but felt the need to support his brother. "I'll admit he's done his fair share of avoiding work over the years, but he is out protecting and serving his country. But the instant he finishes his tour and comes home, all bets are off."

"Damn straight," MD and Sloan both grumbled.

Daniel's phone dinged and he turned it so the other two could see a picture of Colin giving them a thumbs-up, and a second picture of him giving them all the finger.

They laughed, then high-fived. "We have a site!"

"Let's get out of here so I can go put in an offer." Daniel locked up the house and three months later Adventure Docs officially opened for business one week before Colin made it home.

Daniel found himself spending more time at the office than at home. He'd be damn glad when Colin could take on some of the work. The good news, business was brisk and doing better than any of them imagined.

More than anything Daniel hated the paperwork that came with the job, and as soon as they could afford it, they'd hire someone to handle it. He leaned back in the office chair and rested his eyes. It was almost six and he still had another hour of paperwork to finish up.

Soft hands massaged the tense muscles in his neck. "I heard a rumor that I have a husband, but since I never see him, I thought I'd come verify it myself."

A smile slid over his face. He relaxed and let her hands work their magic. "Is that a fact? Just who is this mysterious man?"

Maggie's sigh sent a whole new tension through him. "As I recall, he's a real looker—not the GQ model material, but that rugged, outdoorsy type that makes me warm inside like a chocolate chip cookie fresh from the oven."

Her fingers worked the knot of muscles in his neck. He dropped his head forward, resting his chin on his chest. "You may have the wrong guy since all I do is paperwork these days."

Her murmur of sympathy eased more tension from him. "You poor baby. Why aren't the other boys doing their part?"

He lifted his head and twisted to see the expression on her face. Definitely sarcasm. He settled his hands on her waist, pulled her onto his lap, and kissed her, then pressed his nose into her neck and inhaled. "I've missed you."

"I've missed you more. Where is everyone?"

"Sloan is covering a surf board competition in California."

"I didn't know Sloan surfed, but I could see him fitting right in as a surfer dude."

Her description drew a chuckle from him. "I hate to burst your bubble, but he doesn't surf. He'll be monitoring the event from a jet ski."

"I can definitely see him doing that. Where's MD?"

"He took a crew to cover a motocross event in Spokane."

"Leaving you stuck with the paperwork."

He'd lost the rock, paper, scissors, earning him the title of paperwork bitch. "Yeah, but the good news is, we're booked out for weeks in advance."

"The bad news is, we never see each other."

"As soon as Colin gets home, that's changing."

Maggie tipped up his chin so they were eye-to-eye. "I'm holding you to that mister. Now, pack it in. It's date night and we're going to dinner, then home for some private time, even if it's just sleeping in each other's arms."

Tension threaded through Daniel. Sleep was something he avoided more and more frequently these days, but holding Maggie in his arms sounded like heaven. He shut down his computer and locked up.

Twilight settled over them as they stepped outside, the nip of spring in the air. "Where's your car?" he asked.

"At home. I ran over so we could ride home together."

Of course she had.

She wiggled her fingers at him. "Give me the keys. I'm driving."

He fished the car keys out of his pocket. "Where are we going?"

"It's a surprise. Just get in the car and relax."

She picked up burgers and fries, then drove them to Eagle Point just as the full moon rose over the Rockies. Maggie grabbed a blanket from the back seat and two bottles of beer.

"Bring the food," she said as she laid out the blanket, then opened one bottle and handed it to him. She popped the cap off of hers, took a long drink, and sighed. "I've got to admit, my brother does make an excellent beer."

Daniel tapped his bottle to hers. "To Liam's beer."

They drank, then dug into the food.

Another sigh, but this time in satisfaction from Maggie. "Nothing better than beer and burgers."

Daniel agreed. He hadn't realized how hungry he was until he started eating.

"And under a full moon. Could we be any luckier?"

The glow of the moon shone over Maggie's upturned face. She held a French fry between her teeth. With a cheeky grin, she offered him a bite.

Daniel helped himself to the French fry and her. He kissed her, his tongue delving into her mouth, savoring the taste of beer and potato.

Maggie wrapped her arms around his neck and pressed her breasts to his chest. "I've missed you so much."

He laid her back on the blanket and stared into her eyes. He sensed a deeper discontent. "Things are going to change as soon as Colin gets home."

Why did his words carry a hollow ring to his ears? How many times had he told her this? The inflection in her eyes told him too many.

He rolled onto his back and stared up at the sky. "I'm sorry. I keep dumping this on Colin's absence." He turned his head to find her watching him. "I am going to make some changes."

Her fingers brushed over his forehead and her eyes darkened. "I know you will, but we both know that's not the only reason you're working such long hours. I know you're not sleeping."

He couldn't talk about this. Not with Maggie, not with anyone. He sat up needing space.

Her fingers brushed down his arm and instantly he was back to the day Ryan died. The air heavy with the scent of blood, dust burned his lungs and eyes. Fury pumped through him—at himself for not saving The Kid, at God for taking him.

He blinked and the past vanished. He was alone with Maggie on the hilltop, fists clenched, body rigid.

"Daniel." She reached out to him, but he pushed to his feet before she could touch him. He couldn't allow that, not until he got a handle on his anger. In the past, he'd been able to control the flashbacks and surges of anger—until now. All he wanted was to unleash the fury raging inside of him and pummel something or someone.

Finally, he regained control and faced her. Concern filled her eyes, but he would make her forget. He pulled her to her feet and pressed her head to his chest.

"I'm sorry. It's been a long day."

She tilted her head to look at him, her eyes solemn. "You know I'm here to listen, to support you."

"I know." He couldn't discuss it with her because the mission had been top secret. "Things are going to change." He was going to change.

She looked ready to press him, but instead she said, "I know you will. In the meantime, why don't you make it up to me, right here, right now."

The heat of her gaze burned deep within him. "Your wish is my command."

He'd missed Maggie's tinkling laughter and soaked it in. "You sound like you've been hanging around Sloan too much," she said.

"I might have picked up a few of his moves."

Maggie put a hand to her hip and gave him that stare she'd always given him and Liam when they tried to tell her she couldn't play with them because she was a girl.

"Well show me what you've learned, Solider Boy."

Her laughter fanned the fire burning inside of him. He leaned in and kissed those pouty lips that beckoned his touch, and a whole lot more. He had everything he needed right here—Maggie.

～

PRESENT DAY...

Maggie's face vanished, and Daniel found himself staring into the eyes of a very angry bull moose. He grabbed Lightning's collar and slowly inched backward, dragging the dog with him.

Bears were considered the dangerous animals out here, but every year more people were seriously injured by moose. Moose, unlike deer, weren't afraid of humans, and they frequently mistook dogs for wolves and attacked.

The bull continued to glare at them as Daniel took another step back. Finally, it turned and meandered down to the river.

Daniel released Lightning and he quickly moved up the trail as fast as he could. When he was a safe distance away, he blew out a sigh of relief.

His heart continued to hammer in his chest the same way it had that night with Maggie on the mountain top, only this was fear, not love causing it to pound so hard.

He missed Maggie. She'd been the sunshine in his life, but after he learned she'd kept Colin's journal from him, he'd been furious. He'd shut down completely, but in truth, he'd pushed her away because he couldn't control the rage.

Their marriage hadn't ended because of Maggie. It was all on him. He'd let go of the only thing that gave his life purpose—Maggie.

11

Maggie stopped to rest and take stock of her situation. She knew the terrain. She ran frequently in this area, but finding the actual trail was nearly impossible after the flooding, especially with an inch of snow covering everything. Her only option—continue down the mountain and hope she made it to the trailhead. But that wouldn't be easy as the dense brush and several fallen trees impeded her efforts. But it was either that or wait to die, and doing nothing wasn't in her DNA.

She pushed to her feet and sucked in a breath when movement sent pain up the back of her thigh. She waited for it to ease before she took a tentative step. Sucking in a breath, she took another step and another, ignoring the pain and concentrating on her end goal as if she were beginning a race.

She put her whole focus on reaching the finish line and the best way to do that was to think about anything but the pain and how far it was to the finish line.

If only that technique had worked with her marriage, but she'd been the only one making an effort. And without Daniel's support it hadn't stood a chance.

~

THREE YEARS, six months ago...

Maggie thought coming home would be an adjustment after living a nomadic life for so long, but with her family and marrying Daniel, it just felt right. In fact, her life felt almost prefect. Her job at Paradise General was a good fit and as close as she could get to the adrenaline rush she'd been on with the World Health Center. She liked the change, the slower pace, and falling asleep in Daniel's arms every night.

Colin's return home had been the only mar in an otherwise idyllic life. He'd arrived just as planned a month ago, but he'd been different, and he'd refused to open up to her or Daniel.

The phone rang. Daniel answered it while stirring the scrambled eggs he was making.

"Hey, bro, what's up?" He dropped the spatula. "Calm down and breathe. The flashback isn't real. You're not in Afghanistan. Look out the window. What do you see?"

Maggie moved to the stove and took over the cooking while Daniel talked to Colin, then refilled her coffee cup.

"That's right it's not desert, and there aren't moose in Afghanistan. What else do you see?"

Daniel's shoulders finally relaxed several minutes later. She scribbled a note to him telling him to invite Colin to go running with them.

He nodded and said, "Come running with us this afternoon."

Maggie got plates out of the cupboard.

"You're not intruding, and Maggie's insisting."

"I am," she called out as she set the plates on the table.

"See?"

She set silverware next to the plates.

"No, she's not going to fuss over you."

Maggie grabbed the phone from him.

"Colin Gregorio, when have I ever said anything to you that wasn't the truth, and when have I ever fussed over you?"

"Never," Colin said.

"And I'm not starting now. Come running with us, then we'll all have dinner together."

"You guys are still newlyweds. I don't want to be a third wheel."

Maggie rolled her eyes. "You aren't. We want you to come, so say yes."

Silence. "Okay."

"Great. We'll pick you up at eleven and be ready for a workout." She handed the phone back to Daniel.

They spoke for several more minutes, then Daniel ended the call and scrubbed a hand over his face.

The toast popped and Maggie buttered it. "Is it just me or does it feel like this was more than just a panic attack. Did something happen over there that's triggering PTSD?" she asked.

Daniel scooped up the eggs. "He hasn't said anything to me about anything happening over there."

Maggie's gaze shot up. Something in his tone gave her pause. "What aren't you saying?"

Daniel shrugged, but she didn't miss the tension across his shoulders.

"You two have always been close. I just thought maybe he confided in you."

She didn't miss the resentment in his tone. "Are you angry with me because Colin and I are friends?"

"You and Colin have always been close—closer than we are in some regards." He set the eggs on the table. "Let's eat before the food gets cold."

Maggie laid a hand on his, preventing him from lifting his fork. "Colin and I are friends just like you and Liam."

His hand tensed beneath her fingers. "I know that, and that doesn't bother me."

"Then what is it?"

He gripped his fork, his knuckles whitening as he looked her directly in the eye. "What bothers me is you open up more with Colin than me. I'm your husband. I want you to share these things with me."

Unreasonable and unwarranted, his anger threw her. He was usually composed and soooo reasonable it made her gnash her teeth.

"I don't intentionally do that."

"I know, but it bothers me."

Maggie gave him a cool stare. "It's not like you're totally open and honest with me either."

"What do you mean?"

"I know you're having nightmares, but you keep hiding it from me. Why? Don't you trust me?"

"I trust you, but there are some things I can't discuss."

"You mean won't. You want me to be more open with you, but you can't reciprocate."

"I can't. The missions were classified." He rose and carried the dishes to the kitchen and began loading the dishwasher.

She crossed over to him. "It hurts that you can't share these nightmares with me. I don't like being shut out."

Daniel blew out a breath and she could see the tension slowly leaving his body. "I'm sorry." He hugged her close, burying his face in her hair. "I wish I could tell you, but I can't."

Maggie squeezed him. "If you can't talk to me, then find someone you can talk to."

He nodded, but she could tell it was to appease her when he changed the subject and suggested they to go hiking instead of running.

She'd let the subject drop for now, but they would revisit it.

While she got dressed, Daniel packed a lunch so they could make a day of it. They picked up Colin, who was living at Adventure Docs until he found an apartment and headed to Canyon Ridge, a favorite place for all of them. The anxious man she'd spoken to on the telephone had transformed into the vibrant, ready-for-anything guy she remembered. But Maggie sensed it was as forced as Daniel's attitude had been earlier.

"Daniel tells me Adventure Docs is doing well."

"It is." Colin launched into all the different directions he planned for their business.

Everything about Colin felt like a show, including his ideas for Adventure Docs. It was as if his continual dialogue was to keep them from asking questions he didn't want to answer.

"Won't you have to hire more people to do all that?" Maggie asked.

Colin stopped and adjusted his pack. "Definitely." He started walking again and Maggie had to pick up her pace to keep up.

"What's the rush?"

"There's something at the top I want to show you guys."

"We've done this hike a million times. What could possibly be new?" Daniel asked.

Colin grinned. "There's always something new—you just have to be open to seeing it."

"Well don't keep us in suspense, tell us what it is," Maggie demanded.

Colin tugged her ponytail. "Still hate surprises, don't you?"

Maggie frowned at him. "Still have to be the star of the show."

"Always."

He set off, leaving Maggie and Daniel to follow.

"Your brother can be so annoying sometimes."

Daniel laughed. "Only sometimes?"

Maggie smiled. "Okay, most of the time."

"That sounds like the Colin I know and love."

∼

AN HOUR later they reached the top and Maggie stopped to catch her breath. Colin had set an Olympic pace, and while she might be in good shape, she wasn't at his level.

Colin dropped his pack and climbed onto his favorite boulder as if he were king of the world, which Maggie was pretty sure he was. He raised both arms into the air in jubilation, the wind ruffling his hair and putting a healthy glow on his cheeks.

His smile was one of pure bliss. "Man, I've missed this place. Don't get me wrong I loved the military, but this is home."

Maggie reached out to Daniel and took his hand, understanding everything Colin was feeling. You didn't know how much a place meant to you until you left it. Maybe that was how you came to appreciate it and the people in it.

Her gaze locked with Daniel's before she looked over at Colin and again she had this sense something was off. Behind the devilish sparkle in his eyes lurked a hollowness, and it scared her.

"So, where is this new thing you have to show us?" Maggie asked.

Colin hopped down from the boulder and waved them over to a crevice. About fifteen feet across was a lush, green meadow with an amazing view, but not particularly unique.

Daniel peered down the gorge to the Serenity River forty feet below strewn with massive boulders. "We've seen this before. What's new about it?"

Colin pointed across the gorge. "See that tree over there?"

Maggie and Daniel nodded.

"Watch this."

Colin dropped his backpack, backed up about twenty feet, and started running.

Maggie waited for him to slow down, but he ran faster. At full speed, he flung himself off the cliff toward a spindly tree on the other side. He struck the trunk with enough force to break ribs, wrapping his arms and legs around it.

He extricated himself from the tree, fist-pumped the air, and threw back his head, shouting, "Hooah," a triumphant grin engulfing his face.

How many times had he done this, perfecting it until he had an audience to share his accomplishment? Maggie shuddered to think, and she kept imagining him missing and plunging to his death.

Colin had always been a daredevil, but this went above and beyond anything he'd ever done when they were kids.

"Well, what do you think?" he called across to them.

Maggie snatched up his bag and jabbed a finger his direction. "You're fuckin' crazy, that's what I think."

She marched down the trail, anger boiling inside her. She'd give him what for when she caught up with him. She glanced over at Daniel who kept pace with her, but he'd been surprisingly silent.

"Your brother is nuts. "He is."

She stopped and stared up at him. "Why are you taking this so calmly? He could have died just now."

"I'm aware. I saw the show."

That was exactly what it had been—a show. But for what purpose? Had it just

been the adventure junkie showing off, or had it been something more—a cry for help?

"That's all you have to say?" Maggie demanded.

"Sometimes actions speak louder than words."

"What do you mean by that?"

Daniel took Colin's pack from her and slung it over his shoulder. "You make him listen with words. I plan to make him listen by knocking him on his ass when I get my hands on him."

Maggie gave Daniel a long look and saw murder in his expression. While she understood his reaction, she'd step between them before Daniel did something he'd regret.

❧

HALFWAY DOWN THE trail they met up with Colin. Daniel rushed at his brother and grabbed him by the shirt. "What the hell is wrong with you? You could have died up there."

Colin laughed off his reaction. "You know what your problem is, Daniel? You always want to play it safe. Life is about taking risks."

Daniel shook him. "That was a hell of a lot more than taking a few risks. That was stupid, and dangerous, and you could have died."

Colin yanked himself free. "Could have, but as you can see, I'm still here. Still alive."

Maggie was filled with the certainty he wished he hadn't succeeded, and it started a tremor deep inside.

She stepped between the two men, her back to Daniel and she gave Colin a hard stare. "Colin, you've always been reckless—but lately, it's as if—"

"As if what?" The affable brother turned belligerent.

"Your behavior is a cry for help."

Colin's anger vanished. "Okay, look, I'm sorry I scared you two. How about if I promise I won't do it again?"

Maggie held her ground, uncertain if his words were genuine or if he was just telling them what they wanted to hear.

The sincerity in his gaze convinced her he meant what he said and she relaxed. "Okay, but if I ever see you do something like that again, I'll knock you out and drag you to the nearest psych ward for evaluation. Do you hear me?"

Something passed through Colin's eyes that looked a lot like hope, but was replaced with contrition.

They hiked back to the car in stilted silence. They dropped Colin off, then they went home to shower and change before meeting back at Adventure Docs for dinner with Colin, Sloan, and MD.

The evening went well until a gunshot echoed and Colin dropped to the ground. He rolled into a ball, his hands pressed over his ears.

"Take cover. Incoming."

Daniel crouched down beside him. "We're here, Colin. You're home, safe and sound."

Colin's eyes darted back and forth. "We're under attack. Take cover." He flattened himself onto the deck.

Maggie kneeled beside him, her chest aching. She wanted to reassure him, but she didn't know how to reach him.

MD and Sloan remained close by offering their support.

"Colin, we're all here for you," Maggie said.

He scrambled away from her until his back hit the side of the house. His eyes were wild and his body trembled violently. "They're coming. I can't stop them. I can't shoot. Noooo."

He jerked back, his face pasty and his eyes vacant. "Don't shoot."

He ducked, and began rocking back and forth, repeating "don't shoot" over and over.

Maggie pressed her hand to Colin's back as Daniel held him, tears streaming down her face. She brushed them aside. "Colin, you're okay. Nobody is going to shoot you."

Colin looked her in the eye, his expression so bleak and hollow it scared her to the depths of her soul. "Not me, the babies. Don't let them shoot the babies."

Babies. Oh God, what had happened over there? The horror she saw in Colin's expression told her everything she didn't want to know.

"It's going to be okay, Colin. We're here for you. I promise you, it's going to get better."

Daniel's eyes locked with Maggie's. The utter helplessness in his expression wrapped around her heart and had her blinking back more tears. She ached for him and Colin, and she desperately wanted to help them both, but didn't know what to do.

Maggie's legs were numb by the time Colin finally stopped shaking. It felt like hours, but in reality it had only been minutes. With Daniel's help she got to her feet, and they led Colin to a chair on the deck. He was calmer, but his eyes remained glazed over and vacant.

MD handed Colin a glass of water, and he took a long drink, then leaned back against the chair and closed his eyes.

Finally, Colin blew out a shaky breath and said, "I need a beer."

Sloan handed him one, and he took a long drink.

"That's more like it. I feel the need to tie one on tonight."

No one disagreed with him, but Maggie thought it was the last thing he needed after what she'd witnessed on the mountain this afternoon. What Colin needed was professional help.

She turned away and went into the kitchen to take a moment to pull herself together. Daniel followed and wrapped his arms around her. She clung to him, the emotions of the past few hours leaving her shaky and on edge.

He led her out to the front porch where they had some privacy.

They sat down on the glider, and Daniel set it to rocking with his foot.

Her body trembled. "What happened to him over there?"

"What did he tell you?"

She watched the breeze sway in the treetops. "Nothing other than just now when he said don't shoot the babies."

Maggie twined her fingers through his and he looked deep into her eyes. "I'm worried about Colin. Something happened over there, and he needs professional help."

"Flashbacks are something we've all gone through," Daniel said.

Fury pumped through her. "So what, just buck up and get through it like a man?"

His silence answered her question.

"What do you call Colin's stunt up on the mountain earlier?"

"Typical Colin behavior."

Maggie blew out a frustrated breath. There was nothing typical about that jump. "I disagree. I think you need to take a hard look at his behavior. He's hurting. He needs professional help to deal with this."

She paused to pull her thoughts together. "Daniel, you told me at breakfast that I don't open up to you like I do with Colin. I want to, but this is a two-way street. You have to do the same. I need you to talk to me, tell me what you're feeling."

He stared up at the darkening sky. "I'm sorry. I can't go there right now."

"Go where?"

"To where Colin was. I'm afraid if I do, I'll—"

"You'll what? End up like Colin?" He said nothing in response. "Keeping it bottled up inside is why Colin is having problems. If you can't talk to me, then you need to talk to someone about it because what I saw just now ate me up inside. I saw some horrible things while I was with World Health Center, but we talked about it, we aired it, and we got through it."

He brushed his fingers over her cheek. "I love you, and it means more than I can say that you're here for me, but I just can't talk about this right now."

She understood that it was painful to discuss, but it hurt that he couldn't open up to her. "I won't force you, but I'm always here for you."

The crisp fall breeze blew over her as Daniel pressed her cheek to his chest and set the chair in motion again. In the past, this would have been an idyllic moment with her husband, but instead a sense of foreboding came over her that left her anxious and unsettled.

~

PRESENT DAY...

In retrospect, that had been the beginning of her becoming aware that Daniel was shutting her out, and she should have recognized it for what it was, but she'd been blinded by what was happening with Colin.

The cold seeped into her, the same as it had every time Daniel turned away from her.

She stopped and studied the snow falling from the sky. She'd made little progress in the past hour. Maybe it was time for a new plan. There was a shelter not far from here—if it hadn't been destroyed by the flooding that would at least provide some protection from the elements until help arrived.

She changed direction and put one foot in front of the other even though all she wanted to do was just give up, but she couldn't. Even without Daniel, she had a full life—a family who loved her, good friends.

She might not have been able to get him to share his feelings with her, but she'd always been able to count on him when she needed help. If only he'd been as willing to share his heart.

12

D arkness hovered, coming earlier because of the gloomy clouds looming overheard. The wind swirled, sending the treetops swaying and an eerie whisper sent a chill over Daniel. His concern for Maggie intensified.

Was she hurt? Was she dressed warmly? Why the hell had she gone hiking on a day like today?

After she'd pulled a hamstring, she'd started taking precautions, and she always took Lightning. But that still didn't ensure her safety.

Lightning stopped and let out a long, low whine.

Daniel rubbed his ears. "What's wrong?"

Forlorn brown eyes stared up at him.

"We're going to find her. I promise." He straightened and stared at a particularly dark cloud that hovered above them that made him think of Colin.

Daniel shook his fist at it. "You can't have her, Colin."

The snow fell harder and Daniel scowled at the dark mass. "You hear me, Colin. I'm not letting you have her."

He started walking, Lightning at his side. He and Maggie might not be married any longer, but he'd be damned if he'd let any harm come to her.

~

Daniel carried a box of Liam's beer. He, Sloan, and MD were helping Liam set up Brother Murphy's for its grand opening next week. He set the box on the bar and found Sloan and MD playing a game of darts.

He started to comment, then stopped when Sloan aimed at the dartboard, hitting a bull's-eye. "I'm telling you, he's a fucking crazy man on a mountain bike. He went over that cliff as if there was a trail and there wasn't anything but air."

MD paused before gathering the darts. "He went off Deadman's Drop?"

Sloan nodded.

"And you didn't follow?"

"Hell, no. Do I look like a fucking idiot?"

MD cocked his head in consideration, and Sloan shoved him. "Throw the damn darts."

MD's first dart went wide and he swore. He threw again and made a triple ring, grunting his approval, and the third landed just outside the bull's-eye.

Sloan pulled the darts from the board and stepped back.

"I think you're full of shit. No one could make that jump and survive," MD said.

Sloan paused before throwing the first dart. "You'd think so, but there's video to prove it."

MD's eyes bugged. "Seriously. I've got to see this."

Sloan tossed his dart, then pulled out his phone. "Colin posted it on YouTube."

Colin? What the hell had his brother done now?

Daniel's pulse accelerated as he stepped closer and watched his brother ride off the edge of the cliff, go airborne for an eternity, then land halfway down the mountain, continuing at breakneck speed before he reached the bottom several miles later, spewing dirt as he came to a stop.

Colin yanked off his helmet, white teeth flashing against his dirt-covered face and released a Hooah that echoed across the mountain.

"I'm going to wipe that damn smile off his face."

Sloan and MD spun around. Sloan started to speak, but Daniel stopped him. "I don't want to hear it. This is between Colin and me."

Lately there had been several heated exchanges between them about the unnecessary risks he took. But this wasn't just about Colin's daredevil hijinks, it was about their business and the fact that these stunts made them look reckless to clients.

Daniel strode out of the bar in search of his brother and found him staring out at the Serenity River.

"Well, this is a first. My brother just staring into the water. I expected you to be planning a jump across or kayaking the rapids, but not anything as mild as this."

Colin made no attempt to stop his brother's tirade, just stood silently staring at him.

When Daniel finally stopped to take a breath, Colin asked, "So I assume this is about the videos I posted."

"Videos! There's more than just you leaping off Deadman's Drop? Do you have a death wish? I think maybe Maggie's right. You do need psychiatric help."

His breath heaved as he stared at Colin.

"Are you finished?"

"For the moment."

"Okay, then listen up. This is my life. You don't have to agree with my choices, but you need to respect them."

Daniel clenched his hands at his sides. What he wanted was to shake his brother until that calm facade changed to some real emotion, but he restrained himself. And in truth, Colin had done nothing that could be construed as suicidal, just bat-crap crazy, and there were plenty of YouTube videos to prove he wasn't alone in his behavior.

Daniel crowded him. "You're my brother. I love you and I care what happens to you. We are also partners and your behavior impacts our business, too. You might hate my butting in, but this isn't just about you."

They glared at each other until Liam called for help hauling in tables. The tension eased when Colin grinned and shouted back that he hoped there was beer in return for all this work. Daniel watched him walk away, knowing this wouldn't be the last time he pulled some crazy stunt.

Colin was behaving like he had a death wish, and Daniel was determined to find out what had changed him, then make him listen to reason. They had a business to consider, but more importantly he was worried about his brother.

∼

TWO DAYS LATER, Daniel found Maggie taking inventory in one of the Adventure Docs vans. He slipped his arms around her and nuzzled the back of her neck.

"Oh *Peter*, that feels wonderful."

He spun her around and gave her a mock glare.

Her eyes danced with amusement. "Daniel, I thought you were someone else."

"Obviously. So, just how often does *Peter* come visit?"

She waved off his question. "Oh, you know, every so often when my husband is too busy to attend to my needs."

Was she joking, or was there a more serious undertone?

Her fingers brushed the tension from his forehead. "You don't have to look so serious. I was only teasing. What are you looking for?"

He pushed aside the irritation. "I wanted to see if you were interested in going hiking on Sunday with Colin."

"Let me check when I go into the hospital, but even if I'm scheduled to work, I'll trade with someone." She gave him a cheeky grin that turned his heart to melted caramel. "They all owe me."

She kissed his cheek, then turned back to the van, but before she could step away he spun her around and gave her a kiss—a full-on attack of lips and tongue that produced plenty of heavy breathing.

When he released her, her breath heaved the same as his.

"Wow, what did I do to deserve that?"

He brushed his thumb over her lower lip. "Not a damn thing. You're my wife, and you put up with me being gone an awful lot. I just wanted to show you how much I appreciate that—appreciate you."

Her smile dazzled him. "Appreciation duly noted."

He turned to leave, but stopped when she called out his name. He turned back to her.

She raised up on tiptoe and pressed her lips to his ear. "I love you, and I'll show my appreciation in precise detail tonight, so don't be late."

His heart thumped soundly against his chest. He didn't care if the whole damn world burned down. He would be home to receive her gratitude in full.

~

DANIEL SHOOK Maggie awake just as dawn painted the sky in faint hues of gray. She grumbled and complained about leaving so early, but he appeased her with coffee and an omelet. His brother joined them for breakfast, and Maggie made her displeasure clear to him as well.

Colin merely smiled and continued to antagonize her, which he would regret when she came fully awake. He gestured to the window. "I love early morning. The air is crisp, the silence is calming and the sunrises are spectacular."

Maggie cocked a jaundiced eye at him. "So are sunsets, and I see plenty of those. I don't see why we couldn't have left at ten."

Colin's brows arched, disappearing into his hairline. "And hike in the heat of the day? That's crazy."

She grunted, which Daniel took as agreement, but clearly she still wasn't pleased with the early morning hike.

He sat between the two to act as arbitrator, which had been his role since they were kids. By the time Maggie downed her second cup of coffee, her eyes were fully opened.

They collected their packs and climbed into Colin's SUV.

Maggie buckled her seatbelt. "So where are we going?"

"I thought we'd hike in to see Feather Ridge Falls."

"Seriously? I love waterfalls." She reached forward to squeeze Daniel's hand, and he wished he'd thought to hike in to see the waterfall. He wanted to be the only guy who put that light in her eyes.

"I've never been there, but I've heard the falls are spectacular—especially in the summer, the water is supposed to be a turquoise blue," Maggie said.

"It is. I go there a lot to just get away and put my thoughts in order." Colin's expression momentarily turned somber as it did often these days, then it vanished so quickly Daniel wasn't certain he'd seen it. He knew Colin was suffering far more than the occasional nightmare and bouts of anger Daniel experienced.

"So how's work at the hospital going? Are you ready to come over to the dark side and work full time for Adventure Docs yet?" Colin asked.

Maggie's laughter filled the interior of the truck. "You wish."

"I do. They're underpaying and under appreciating you, isn't that right, bro?"

Daniel held up his hands. "I'm not getting involved in this."

"Coward."

Daniel grinned. "Nope, just a happily married man who intends to stay that way. You want to stir the pot and piss off the queen bee, go for it."

Maggie's eyes narrowed. "Queen bee. Are you implying I'm a prima donna?"

"Don't put words in my mouth. I'm just saying where you work is up to you. That's all."

A look passed between Colin and Maggie that told him he'd been played. But that didn't bother him nearly as much as the silent connection between his brother and wife. They spoke on a level that transcended words. It was a connection he and Maggie didn't have and he desperately wanted.

～

MAGGIE AND COLIN followed Daniel into the tunnel behind Feather Ridge Falls. Damp, musty air filled the confined space as they crossed slick, moss-covered rocks.

Stepping out of the tunnel, a heavy mist soaked Daniel's face as he watched the hundred and fifty foot fall plunge into the punch bowl-shaped basin of turquoise water.

Hot and sweaty, they dropped their backpacks on the sandy beach and ate their lunch.

Maggie finished her sandwich and sighed. "It doesn't get much better than this—a hike to a stunning waterfall, good food, and a nap." She settled back against Daniel.

"Aw come on. Let's go swimming," Colin said.

Maggie gave him a cool look. "A little too chilly for my tastes."

"What about you, bro?"

Daniel patted his stomach. "Sorry, I just ate."

"That's an old wives' tale, and you only had a nutrition bar."

It might be true, but Daniel would use it as an excuse. "What are you, three? You don't need me to swim with you." Daniel wrapped an arm around Maggie and pulled her snug against his chest.

Colin swore and headed to the water.

Maggie looked up at him. "You don't have to stay with me."

"The hell I don't. I'm not putting so much as a toe into that iceberg."

Maggie's soft laugher drifted over him as she closed her eyes. "I knew I married an intelligent man."

Daniel's eyes grew heavy, and he'd been on the verge of falling asleep when a rock splashed into the water.

He looked up and found Colin teetering on a ledge high above the water.

Daniel scrambled to his feet and shouted, "What are you doing?"

Colin shot him a cocky grin. "Diving." He plunged into the water, and an instant later he surfaced and swam to the shore where Daniel stood.

"What the hell were you thinking? There are all kinds of boulders in here. Do you even have any idea how deep it is? You could have killed yourself."

For an instant, Daniel swore he saw a flash of disappointment before Colin shook the water from his face and walked past him without responding.

Daniel grabbed his arm. "What the hell is going on with you?"

"Nothing's going on." He shook off Daniel's hand and began putting on his boots. "We should get going. I have things to do at the office."

Maggie gaped at him while he finished tying his boot, then pushed to his feet. "You two are just being a couple of worrywarts. I'm a big boy, and I can take care of myself." He slipped on his pack. "I'll see you at the car."

Daniel watched him disappear down the trail, then turned to Maggie. "What the hell was that about?"

"I don't know, but I don't like it. He keeps taking more and more risks, and he's scaring me." She leveled a hard stare at him. "And don't you dare tell me I'm overreacting because we both know I'm not."

Daniel blew out a weary breath. "You're right. His behavior is becoming more reckless. MD and Sloan showed me a video of Colin going off Deadman's Drop."

Maggie face went white. "On his bike?"

"Yeah, even Sloan and MD thought he was crazy."

"That's bad—really bad."

Daniel agreed. If MD thought his behavior was risky, it was, because MD took more risks than all of them combined.

Maggie tugged on a boot. "He's been different ever since he came home. I keep asking him what's wrong, but he tells me everything is fine. Clearly everything is *not* fine."

Daniel nodded his agreement. He would talk to him again and this time he would get answers.

～

PRESENT DAY...

But he never got answers. Colin had continued to insist he could handle it on his own and Daniel had let it go. He should have pushed harder, but in truth, pressing Colin to get help would have forced Daniel to take a hard look at his own problems.

Daniel stopped and took a drink of water, while Lightning drank deeply from a nearby puddle. He dug into his pack and pulled out a bag of biscuits he always kept for emergencies and fed one to the dog.

The wind kicked up, and the snow fell harder. A flash of red fluttered through a thick cluster of pine trees.

Daniel pushed his way through them to discover what he'd seen were a few remaining brilliant red leaves clinging to a maple tree.

Lightning nosed the ground, his tail wagging furiously. Suddenly he stopped, his tail pointing straight out as he sniffed a piece of material caught on a pine tree fluttering in the breeze.

Daniel plucked the fabric from branch, then studied the ground. An impression of a jogging shoe was buried in the mud.

Someone had been here.

Lightning barked and jetted up the trail. Daniel followed. His heart accelerated and hope surged. Someone had been here. Please let it have been Maggie.

Moving forward became more and more difficult. Every step took energy and effort from Maggie's already depleted resources. She kept moving using the same inner strength she drew on for running, but instead of reaching the finish line, her goal was to find shelter.

She dug deep, searching for the fortitude to continue. She'd done triathlons that took every bit of her strength and she could do this, even with the hamstring injury slowing her down.

But she'd learned determination alone wasn't always enough. Sometimes she didn't finish a race no matter how much she wanted to persevere. Determination hadn't salvaged her relationship with Daniel, either. If only she'd acted when she first saw it start to unravel.

~

Two years, one month ago...

Maggie rolled over and found Daniel's side of the bed empty, the clock on his nightstand read midnight. She got out of bed and followed the muted light into the living room where she found him watching television in the dark.

She slipped her arms around him and he tensed. Any other time she'd have written it off, but with Colin's behavior fresh in her mind she couldn't.

She sat down on the sofa so she could see his expression, and she didn't like what she saw. The pallor, the tension, the emptiness in Daniel's eyes. "What's wrong?"

He stared at her with vacant eyes, then shrugged. "Nothing. I couldn't sleep."

"This isn't nothing. You had another nightmare, didn't you?"

He stilled, his shoulders bunching and his hand gripping the water glass. "What makes you think that?"

An incredulous laugh slipped over her lips. "You're kidding, right? Look at you. You're wound up so tight you're about to snap."

Anger flashed in his eyes, then disappeared along with the tension in his body. He blew out a weary breath. "It's nothing. I'm just having trouble going to sleep."

"Like Colin."

The anger returned hot and furious. "No, not like Colin. I'm not pulling dangerous stunts."

"No, you're not, but you're not sleeping and you're on edge a lot more frequently."

"Because of work."

Work was a handy excuse. Lately, she'd begun to suspect he used it as an excuse to avoid her, but she couldn't deny he'd been under a lot of pressure that hadn't eased as much as she'd hoped with Colin's return.

His eyes softened and he tugged her to him. "I'm sorry. We're interviewing assistants this week and that will lighten my load."

Everything he said made perfect sense, but instinct told her there was more he wasn't telling her.

He kissed her and she forgot everything but him and her body's response to his touch. And maybe that's exactly what he'd intended.

❧

THE NEXT MORNING, Maggie met Colin for their Friday morning hike at six. Rubbing the sleep from her eyes, she sipped her coffee. Why did everyone insist on dragging her out of bed at dawn?

Colin greeted her with a chipper grin. "You've never been a morning person, have you?"

"Never, and your disgustingly cheerful attitude is not appreciated. And just for the record, some of us work late hours and need our sleep."

Colin raised his arms toward the sunshine bursting over the horizon. "Be honest, wouldn't you rather be here to experience the sunrise than sleeping?"

She couldn't deny it was a glorious view, and with some caffeine in her system she was beginning to feel human, but her competitive streak wouldn't allow Colin to think he'd won this round.

So, instead of agreeing with him, she said, "Let's get this show on the road."

Colin's smug grin told her he knew the truth. She ignored it and grabbed her pack, leaving her empty coffee cup in the car and they set off.

She and Colin had made a climb at least once a month since he'd returned from Afghanistan, but this would most likely be their last climb for the season as snow would make the trails impassable in the winter.

Pine Ridge was not a trail for beginners, and today it was more treacherous than usual with the dusting of snow from the night before. Colin pushed on without the slightest hesitation and Maggie followed, but not with the same abandonment.

They reached the top two hours later, clouds beginning to fill the sky, but not enough to block the view of Paradise Falls all the way to the Canadian border.

"Okay, I admit this was worth crawling out of bed before dawn to see. It's spectacular."

Colin climbed onto an icy boulder that overlooked the valley below and raised his arms high toward the heavens, shouting, "Hooah" as he'd done on each of their hikes.

His voice reverberated across the valley. He raised a leg, balancing precariously, his expression pinched. Before Maggie could ask what was wrong, he slipped. Arms flailing, he tried to regain his balance.

"Colin!" Maggie scrambled to grab a fistful of his jacket and yanked, sending them both tumbling to safety.

"What the hell did you do that for? You could have gotten hurt."

Could have? Maggie took inventory of her cuts and scrapes and determined she'd have plenty of aches and pains for her efforts.

"You're welcome for saving your ass."

"My ass didn't need saving. I was doing fine."

"You were doing fine if you intended to fall off that boulder and plunge to your death."

The resulting silence was as unsettling as the expression on Colin's face that said falling a thousand feet to his death wouldn't have been a bad thing.

"Are you trying to kill yourself?"

His features darkened with anger. "Don't be ridiculous. Why would I want to do that?"

Maggie considered his comment for a long moment. "You tell me."

"I wouldn't."

His denial didn't ring true. "I don't believe you."

His expression turned serious. "I wasn't trying to kill myself."

"So you keep saying, but your behavior feels like a cry for help."

"It's not."

She didn't miss the irritation in his tone.

"I'm not a child, Maggie, and I'd appreciate it if everyone stopped treating me like one."

"Then stop behaving like a ten-year-old."

They glare at each other, then Colin grinned at her and that old teasing twinkle came into his eyes. It was the old Colin again. "Have I ever lied to you?"

She wanted to continue the conversation, but she could see she wouldn't get anywhere, so she followed his lead. "Yes, plenty of times."

"Name one," Colin demanded.

"The time you told me that if I flapped my arms hard enough I could fly off the shed roof. I ended up with a broken leg, thanks to you."

His deep laughter boomed. "You were pretty gullible back then."

"I was only five."

"Excuses, excuses. Name something else."

Maggie gave him a cool look. "What about when you convinced me there was a monster in old Mr. Tucker's backyard that turned out to be a giant St. Bernard, and that dog didn't have a mean bone in his body?"

Colin's grin was as piercing as the sunlight angling through the clouds. "Okay, so maybe I told you a teeny, tiny fib that time."

"No maybe about it. And it wasn't a fib—it was a flat-out lie."

"That's a little harsh, don't you think?"

"No, I do not. I had nightmares for months because of you."

Their bickering continued all the way down the trail and it felt like old times, but that look on Colin's face was burned into Maggie's consciousness. Had he wanted to fall?

~

MAGGIE ARRIVED home and worked in the garden until late afternoon, then showered and dressed to meet Daniel for dinner at her brother's pub. She opted to ride her bike the three miles instead of taking her car.

She reached Brother Murphy's and studied the exterior.

Quaint.

Liam would hate the description, but that was what it was. He may have wanted a manly Irish Pub, but painting the exterior in soft creams with clusters of flowers under the windows and lining the walkway made it quaint and inviting. And the gurgle of the river flowing past the back deck, only added to the charm and appeal.

She parked her bike inside the kitchen.

"Hey, this isn't a storage unit," her brother grumbled.

"Then get some bike racks so your customers have a place to park their bikes."

"I'm working on it, but until then you can work off your parking fees."

"Not likely. I'm meeting my husband for dinner." She started for the pub, but Liam's next words stopped her mid-stride.

"Would that be the same husband pouring drinks behind the bar?"

With a sinking heart, Maggie peeked out the door and saw Daniel filling a pitcher of beer. "You make it damn hard to come here and relax."

"Don't blame me. You're the one who talked me into opening this place." He tossed her an apron. "I'm short a waitress."

She shot her brother a dark look while she tied on the apron, regretting that she'd ever encouraged him. She left the kitchen without a word and stepped behind the bar to grab a pencil and order pad.

She cozied up to Daniel. "Why did you let him rope you into working?"

He turned, a smile on his face as he gave her a slow perusal that made her forget her ire with Liam and want to drag Daniel home where they could have some privacy for a repeat of last night.

"He offered me the family and friends deal, and I couldn't turn it down. I'm guessing you got trapped into working, too."

Maggie tried to maintain her outrage, but couldn't because it had taken little effort on her brother's part to coerce her into helping him. Her lower lip extended. "I hate smug men."

Daniel's grin turned devious as he leaned in close. "I'm calling bullshit. You married one, so you can't hate them too much." His lips settled over hers, and she forgot everything but him.

"Hey, break it up. This is a respectable pub, not a place for public displays of affection, especially from employees."

Maggie gazed over at her brother. "We are not employees. We were bullied into filling in for you."

"You weren't badgered, harassed, or even pestered. I just pointed out only waitresses park their bike in my kitchen." He nodded his head toward the dining room. "Table four is waiting."

"Smugness does not become you," she muttered as she left the bar and went to take orders.

~

THE COZY, intimate meal with Daniel didn't materialize until after closing, but Liam prepared them a special dinner they ate in front of the fire pit in the center of the deck.

"So, how was your hike today?"

Maggie's brow furrowed. "Disturbing."

Daniel set his fork down and gave her his full attention. "What happened?"

Maggie tried to decide where to begin. "We hiked up to Pine Ridge, and the trail was dusted with snow, but we made it up in two hours."

"That's a pretty good pace."

"It was and at the top Colin found a boulder and did his usual victory arm pump."

She paused and Daniel prompted her. "What happened?"

Maggie waved a hand in dismissal, her concerns seemed silly now.

He stroked her cheek. "Tell me."

She could never resist him. "I think I'm overreacting, but then he raised up on one foot and—"she closed her eyes recalling the terror she'd felt in that instant"—he slipped. I grabbed him, but for a moment, the look on his face made me think he'd wanted to fall."

Daniel's expression went blank.

"I know it's crazy. Colin would never do that. An instant later it was gone, and he was giving me a hard time for overreacting." She chewed on her lower lip. "You think I'm overreacting, too, don't you?"

His silence disturbed her more than the thoughts she'd been struggling with all day. "Tell me you think I'm crazy, that Colin would never—"

Daniel squeezed her hand. "No, I don't think Colin would harm himself, but his demons are getting to him, even Sloan and MD have commented on it. He's different. I've asked him, but he keeps telling me everything is fine. Everything is *not* fine."

The food Maggie had eaten soured in her stomach. The idea that Colin would actually harm himself was unthinkable. "I think we should get a professional opinion."

Daniel stared into the fire a long moment, then nodded.

Maggie pressed her head to his shoulder, anxiety replacing her appetite. She just prayed that gave them some insight into what was going on with Colin and how to help him.

~

PRESENT DAY...

They didn't get Colin the help he needed in time, and Maggie would forever regret that.

The trail took a steep incline. Maggie leaned heavily on her stick as she walked through the slush and mud. She paused after climbing over a downed tree not sure she had the energy to continue.

Colin's face appeared through the snow, the glow sending light and warmth over her.

You can do this.

His image vanished, but his encouragement gave her the push she needed to keep going. She would get out of this mess. She wouldn't give up. She would survive.

14

Daniel shouted Maggie's name. His voice momentarily echoed before the wind carried it off.

No response.

MD spoke into his com. "Daniel, we're being asked to move the van to Pineapple Run where they're starting another search."

They'd lose their com connection and have to rely on their cell phones. "Take the van over. I'm staying here to search for Maggie."

"Copy that. Any sign of her?" MD asked.

"Nothing yet. I'm going to come down Twilight Ridge." They both knew it was one of Maggie's favorite trails.

"Let me know if you find her."

"Copy that."

Daniel ignored all the odds stacked against her if she'd been caught in a flash flood and focused on the fact she was a survivor. She never gave up, and if there was a breath left in her body, she would continue fighting. She'd been relentless with Colin, too, trying everything to get him to help. If only he'd listened to her sooner, but he'd convinced himself his brother would work though his problems on his own. He'd never been more wrong.

~

Daniel loaded his backpack, grabbed his mountain biking shoes, then headed to the truck. Maggie tossed her pack into the back seat.

"I thought you weren't riding today?"

"I'm not. I'm going to run instead, but I can take my car if this is a guy outing."

Daniel slid his arms around her and kissed the tip of her nose. "You're always welcome. You're one of the guys."

Maggie leaned back, scrunching her nose. "I'm not sure I consider that a compliment."

Daniel gave her a slow once over. "It is." He tugged her closer. "You're one of the guys, but with much better features."

She arched a brow at him. "You sound like you're describing a car."

"If I were, it would be a sleek, expensive model that hugged the road and fit me like a glove."

His description produced a laugh from her. "Only you could make comparing me to a car come off as a compliment."

Laughter rumbled in his chest. "We could skip the outing and stay here. I could show you in exact detail what I like about you."

She swayed closer to him. "You had your chance earlier, but then you dragged me out of bed before daylight, and if I have to be up at this ungodly hour, we're going."

She spun around, leaving him throbbing and wanting her more than ever. How he ever got so lucky to win the heart of a woman like her, he didn't have a clue, but he would do everything in his power to make her happy. Except talk to her. But he couldn't tell her what happened to Ryan.

They met Colin at the trailhead to Twilight Ridge and Daniel unloaded his bike, while Maggie put on her running shoes.

"Where's Maggie's bike?" Colin asked as he dropped the tailgate and lifted out his bike.

"She decided to run instead of bike."

"Can't keep up with the boys, Mags?" Colin called over to her.

"In your dreams. If I were riding, you'd be eating my dust."

"Kind of hard to prove that since you're not riding."

Maggie tied her shoe then came around so she was toe-to-toe with Colin. "How many miles are you planning on riding today?"

Colin shrugged. "I don't know ten, fifteen. We're doing the ridge ride."

"Okay, so you do that, and I'll do a fifteen-mile run on the lower Twilight Trail. The first one back here wins."

"There's no way you can beat us."

Daniel didn't miss the twinkle in her eyes, and he decided then and there he would never bet against her because it was a losing proposition—on all counts, especially for him.

She stood feet braced, hands on hips, chin tilted, and taunted his brother. "Bawk, bawk, bawk."

Colin held up a hand. "Okay, what's the bet?"

Maggie tapped her finger against her chin, then offered up a devious smile. "Winner buys drinks at Brother Murphy's."

Colin thought a minute, then held out his hand. "Deal." He turned to Daniel. "You in?"

"Hell, no. It's a losing bet."

Colin's cocky grin flashed. "I know, but I can't turn down free beer."

Daniel shook his head. "It's not a losing bet for Maggie, you moron. She's going to win."

Colin's confident expression flickered, then his resolve returned. "There's no way she can beat our bikes."

Daniel studied the trail up the ridge. "Yeah, you keep telling yourself that, but if there's one thing I know about my wife, she wouldn't make that bet unless she was damn certain she could win. So, you go ahead, but my money's on you eating crow when we get back here."

Colin grunted, turned on the camera attached to the top of his helmet, then strapped on the helmet. "Let's get this show on the road." He grinned at Maggie. "I'll be kicking back and waiting for you when you get done."

"In your dreams, Biker Boy." She snapped on her hydration pack. "Why don't you call now and reserve a seat for me?" Her laughter trailed after her as she set off.

Colin set a brutal pace, which didn't surprise Daniel as his brother hated to lose, which wouldn't have been a problem if the trail were in better shape, but they had to stop and lift their bikes over fallen trees, making the ride twice as long. He suspected Maggie had known that when she made the bet.

The trail took a steep incline and Daniel pedaled hard to keep up with his brother. His bike spun out on the graveled surface several times, but he made it to the top where Colin waited for him.

"Maggie set us up."

Daniel sucked in air, shaking his head. "Wrong. She set *you* up. I didn't bet."

Colin scowled at him, then grinned. "I know a shortcut."

"What's the condition of the trail?"

"It can't be any worse than this."

Famous last words. The shortcut made the trail they'd been on seem like freshly paved road.

They stopped a mile later in the middle of a small meadow, both winded and sucking in air. "I vote we go back," Daniel said.

"If we do that, I'll lose the bet."

"You've already lost the bet. There's no way you can win no matter which trail you take now."

Colin's laughter echoed across the field. "It ain't over until the fat lady sings," he said, then set off.

Daniel seriously contemplated going back. He wanted to ride, not constantly fight debris on the trail. In the end, he followed, deciding it couldn't get any worse.

Wrong.

The trail narrowed and became steeper. A mile later, they reached the top. Colin bellowed out a triumphant shout and fist pumped the air. "It's all downhill from here. There's no way she can win."

Daniel checked the time. Maggie ran ten-minute miles on average so it should take her around two hours to finish her run. They were already an hour and a half into their ride. It would be close, damn close.

"Just because it's all downhill doesn't mean you need to go forty miles an hour."

"What would be the fun in going slow?"

Daniel liked downhill as much as the next guy, but he considered it a good ride when he made it to the bottom in one piece. This trail was steep, strewn with fallen trees, deep ruts and wicked rocks. Before he could make another objection, Colin careered down the mountain without a second thought.

Daniel followed him, but maintained a more moderate pace—still too damn fast for his comfort as they moved into a series of switchbacks.

Halfway down, the trail took a sharp turn, leading into a long, vertical downhill.

A fallen tree blocked the trail. As if in slow motion, he watched Colin hit a rut, throwing him off-balance. He went airborne. A limb caught the spoke and ripped the bike out from under him, hurtling him over the side of the mountain.

Daniel braked hard, his back tire coming off the ground. He dropped his bike and scrambled down the ledge, nausea building in his throat. He found Colin clinging to a tree dangling over the ledge —the only thing between him and a hundred-foot free-fall.

Dropping to his belly, Daniel inched toward him, dirt and gravel crumbling beneath him. "Take my hand."

Colin looked up at him, but he didn't reach out. "Get back before you fall."

"Don't be a fool. Take my arm and I'll pull you up."

The tree shifted and dropped Colin lower. "No, get back." Dirt and gravel tumbled down the sheer drop.

Daniel inched forward and stretched out his arm. "I'm not letting you fall. Take my arm."

When Colin didn't respond, Daniel leaned over farther, hoping the tree wouldn't shift again and send them both to their deaths. He grabbed Colin's hand and started pulling. More gravel and dirt tumbled out from underneath him.

A groan echoed just before the trunk split.

Daniel held tight to his brother.

"Let me go," Colin shouted.

"I can't do that."

Colin looked down, then into Daniel's eyes. "I can."

"No, don't."

Colin's eyes darkened with regret and something Daniel thought looked like relief. "I love you."

Daniel tightened his grip. "Hang on to me. Don't give up."

"I can't do it any more. I'm sorry." Colin's hand went slack.

Daniel grabbed for him, but only got air. He squeezed his eyes shut, tears leaking from under his eyelids. He got on his bike and tore down the trail praying for a miracle.

～

MAGGIE REACHED THE TRAILHEAD, and bent forward leaning her hands on her thighs as she sucked in air. A good run. She'd pushed hard, because no way was she letting the guys win.

She heard the bikes coming before she saw them. She raised her arms and started her victory dance.

Daniel flew past her and skidded to a stop. "Come on," he shouted racing to the truck. He grabbed the medical kit from under the backseat.

"What's wrong?"

"Colin fell."

Maggie's stomach plummeted as she sprinted after Daniel, dodging downed trees and brush.

They found Colin about a quarter mile from the trailhead and Daniel called 9-1-1 back giving them their location, then handed her the phone as he opened his medical kit.

Maggie dropped to her knees beside Colin and applied pressure to the blood gushing from his forehead.

Colin's eyes fluttered open and his lips quirked. "I really did it this time, Mags."

"Shush. We're here. Don't worry, everything is going to be fine." She glanced over at Daniel as he worked to stop the bleeding from Colin's stomach. As soon as he had it under control, he took the phone from her and stepped away to report on Colin's injuries.

"Mags." Colin's voice was barely a whisper of sound and his eyes were glazed over.

She leaned closer so she could hear him. "Yes."

"My journal's in my nightstand. Burn it. Don't—don't want Daniel to read it." His fingers gripped her wrist. "Promise me." He arched up, his face contorting with pain. "Promise me," he gasped out again.

"I'll take care of it."

His grip eased and his breathing slowed, then stopped altogether. "Colin!"

She began CPR. "Daniel, he's not breathing."

Maggie prayed for a miracle as she and Daniel worked side-by-side to save his brother, but she knew it was pointless. Colin was gone.

~

LIAM OFFERED to shut down Brother Murphy's for Colin's wake, and Daniel and his father accepted the offer. It was the perfect location to celebrate Colin's life. In fact, it was the kind of place his brother would have chosen if he'd had a vote.

Daniel crossed over to where Sloan and MD were swapping stories about Colin. "Hey, remember when we took that trip down the Snake River and—"

Boisterous laughter circulated through the group and Daniel joined in remembering the trip clearly, but the hollowness inside reminded him that all he had left were stories of his brother. There would be no new adventure for him and Colin to share. No lively chatter first thing in the morning at work. They would never grow old together, never fight or argue again. He needed more than memories to sustain him in the days and weeks and years to come.

Sloan pulled him from his musings. "Hey Daniel, tell us about the time you and Colin did that fly fishing challenge."

A bittersweet smile eased the pain in his chest as he told the story to a group of Colin's ranger buddies.

"I can't believe he hooked your lip with that fly," Sloan said.

"I've got the scar to prove it." Daniel pulled out his lower lip and received a round of Atta boys. Colin's friends appreciated his battle scars the same as he and Colin had.

He searched the room for Maggie, needing the warmth of her smile, the touch of her hand.

He found her in the far corner of brew house, but when he started toward her instead of the welcoming smile he'd expected, she frowned and his step faltered. She'd been his rock since he'd found her cradling Colin's broken body in her arms at the bottom of the ravine. She'd been there for him, holding him, comforting him even though it was his fault Colin was dead.

The all-too-familiar guilt resurged. He hadn't protected his brother as he'd promised his mother and that would forever haunt him.

He almost wished Maggie would throw condemnations at him instead of love and affection. He relished the idea of punishment. Maybe then he would find absolution.

He reached her side and nodded to the man she spoke to.

"Paul, this is my husband, Daniel Gregorio. Daniel this is Paul Crandall, an old army buddy of Colin's."

Daniel shook the man's hand, then slipped his arm around Maggie. The subtle tension in her shoulders made him wonder if his touch was welcome, but he selfishly held on anyway. He needed to lean on her, feel the steady grounding of her presence. Having her by his side was the only thing that kept him sane.

"It's a pleasure to meet you," he said to Paul and meant it, but he needed a private moment with his wife away from everyone, especially the dozens of media vans that crowded the tiny town of

Paradise Falls. They'd hounded Daniel, Maggie, and his father for comments about the man they'd loved and lost.

How Colin had dealt with the fame and being under the constant scrutiny of the world during his baseball days, Daniel would never know, but he'd taken it in stride. He'd always been his true self, never caring what anyone thought. He'd been genuine, and it was why he'd been beloved by his fans who mourned his retirement from baseball and now his death.

Paul made a few more comments then left to refill his beer. Daniel used the opening to suggest they step out on the deck. He wanted a private moment, and they certainly wouldn't find it in here.

He led her outside and they took the few steps toward the river where fewer people were gathered.

A wobbly sigh slipped from her lips. "I knew this would be hard, but it's so much more difficult than I expected."

Daniel tightened his arms around her, but she still held herself back. "I know." He glanced across the river where the cluster of media vans waited to pounce on the slightest tidbit of news about Colin like a starving dog. He resented their presence. He didn't want their grief turned into a public spectacle like some reality television show.

He turned his back on them and buried his face in the crook of Maggie's neck. "It's so hard having our every move followed, being on display for the world to see."

Maggie nodded. "Colin wouldn't have liked it, but he'd have known how to deal with them."

Her ragged inhale tore at his composure. "I'm sorry, Maggie."

She abruptly pulled back and looked at him. "Sorry for what?" He started to respond, and she shook a finger at him. "Don't you dare blame yourself for his death. It was not your fault."

"But—"

"No buts. NOT. YOUR. FAULT."

Her gaze didn't waver, and he believed her. "Then what was going on inside? You didn't seem to want me to touch you."

Her face softened, and she brushed a hand over his cheek. "That wasn't about you. That was about me trying to hold it together in public. I knew the moment you touched me I'd fall apart, and I don't want to do that here."

His shoulders relaxed. He could survive this, so long as he had Maggie's support.

"And the frown when I came over to you just now?"

"Paul was telling me a story about one of Colin's crazy stunts that I didn't want you to hear."

She'd been protecting him. Another surge of relief went through him, and he smiled. "You think I don't know about those stories? I've been hearing them all day."

Her smile wavered. "I know you have, and I didn't want you to have to endure another one."

He pressed a kiss to her forehead. "Tell me we're going to make it through this?"

Another ragged breath. "We are, but—" Her voice broke and a shudder passed through her. Tears pooled in her eyes. "Could we do this at home where hundreds of people aren't watching?"

He nodded and pulled her close, absorbing her softness, the warmth of her skin, the sweet scent of her hair. "Yes."

"Thank you." Her voice whispered over him, and he thought just maybe he'd survive.

~

PRESENT DAY...

Losing Colin had sent him over the edge. The nightmares switched from Ryan to Colin and the anger intensified. Instead of leaning on Maggie, he'd turned away from her and buried himself in work so that he didn't lash out at her.

Distancing himself from Maggie had also been a way to punish himself. He didn't deserve forgiveness, and he sure as hell didn't deserve Maggie. So he'd put more space between them when all he'd wanted was to fall into her arms.

15

The temperature plummeted. The cold seeped into Maggie's body. Every step expended more energy. Uncontrollable shivers shook her so hard she stumbled and fell.

What if she just stayed on the ground and stopped fighting? Remaining where she was meant certain death. She could relax. She could let go like Colin had.

Move!

She pushed to her feet.

"I-I-I'm not a quitter," she said aloud.

You're a champion, Mags.

Colin's voice came to her as clearly as if he stood beside her rooting her on.

Never stop trying, never quit. Screw second. Just do it.

The motivations made her smile and she reached deeper. She could do this. She would survive. She would find shelter.

She pulled out every motivational trick she used when exhaustion goaded to quit during a race.

Go for the gold. Go big or go home. If you think big, you'll be big.

But this was more than a race—this was her life and the biggest challenge she'd ever faced. One she couldn't lose. Unlike Daniel.

She'd been disloyal to him, but she'd been torn between keeping her promise to Colin and lying to her husband. Colin had begged her not to let Daniel see his journal. After she retrieved it and read it, she'd been torn between keeping her promise to Colin and showing it to Daniel. And while she debated what to do, Daniel found the journal.

No matter how she'd tried to explain what she'd done, a yawning canyon opened that neither of them could cross. When they stopped talking and touching, she'd realized it was over, but when he'd made no attempt to stop her from leaving, it shattered her.

~

TWO YEARS AGO...

"How could you keep this from me?" Daniel's gaze darkened with reproach as he shook Colin's journal at her.

She met his anger head on, hating Colin for putting her in this position. "I promised Colin."

Hurt and anger burned in his eyes. "Even from me."

The lump in her throat grew until she could only whisper the words. "Especially you."

"Why?" The anguish in his voice cut through her.

"I don't know." Resolved to confess everything, she prayed he'd understand. "When I was holding him just before he died, he told me he was sorry about what had happened in Afghanistan, and he asked me to destroy his journal."

He held out the section she'd read time and again and knew by heart. "This was more than just some random journal entry."

"I know that." Colin's pain and guilt had tormented her, and his words were burned into her memory.

We were out on a mission, a small village that had harbored insurgents in the past. We were searching the houses when a mother and young boy walked down the street toward us. I ordered them to stop, but they kept coming. I had orders to shoot if they didn't stop. I yelled at them again and aimed at the mother. My commander was shouting into my com shoot them both. I couldn't do it. Then Bobby Delgado came out of the house he'd been searching. One minute everything was calm, the next, all hell broke loose when the mother detonated the bombs strapped to her and the boy. Shoot a baby or lose Bobby. Everyone died because I did nothing.

"You didn't think I had a right to know about this?" He shook the journal at her. "It explains his behavior."

Recrimination hung in the air.

Maggie stared at him, searching for the words to explain her actions, but came up empty.

"Don't you have anything to say?"

Her response sounded lame even to her ears. "He begged me not to tell you, and what good would it have done. He was already dead."

"Why didn't you just burn it?"

"I started to several times, but then I just couldn't without showing it to you."

"But you didn't show it to me."

A thick silence filled the room.

"No. I-I didn't want to hurt you."

"So you just let me find it on my own."

The pain in his voice tore her up inside. Maggie reached out to comfort him, but he drew back. A slap to the face would have been less painful.

"That wasn't my intent."

"But that's what happened."

She couldn't deny the truth of his words.

His eyes burned with a fury she'd never seen before, and in that moment, she knew she'd lost him—that he would never forgive her. No explanation would change the fact she'd kept this from him even if it was to protect him. Her actions also gave him another excuse to pull away from her. He'd worked long hours since Colin died, and while she'd tried to reach out to him, he kept his pain inside—just like Colin had done.

"I don't know what else to say except I'm sorry."

"Not good enough."

His stone-cold expression held no mercy, no forgiveness, not an ounce of compassion. He stared at her a long moment, then turned away.

She fled to the bedroom, closed the door and sat on the bed. Her stomach ached from holding back the tears, but she kept them bottled up inside until the front door slammed. She waited until Daniel's headlights disappeared, then the floodgates burst, and she cried until there was nothing left inside.

She crawled into bed and rolled into a tight knot of misery.

She'd lost Colin, and now Daniel—one to death and one to deception.

~

PRESENT DAY...

Maggie made it through those dark days after losing Colin by leaning on friends and family. It wasn't what she'd wanted, but Daniel left her no choice when he turned away from her.

Through it all she'd never stopped wanting him, loving him.

The trail forked to the left. She paused to suck in air before continuing. Why hadn't someone invented a surefire cure to heal a broken heart?

Maggie pushed the thought aside and hobbled forward. She rounded a bend and not fifty yards away, a shelter came into view.

The pain and fatigue were momentarily forgotten with the enticement of shelter and warmth. She limped forward. It certainly wasn't ideal as it only had a roof and no sides, but there was a fire pit and a stack of wood ready to light.

She searched through her bag and found a lighter. She finally managed to get
it to work and got the fire started. She huddled next to it, praying someone found her soon before the cold won the race.

16

The howl of a mountain lion set off a low rumble in Lightning's chest, and his hackles rose. The hair prickled on Daniel's neck as he searched through the thick knot of trees that closed in around them like a snug cocoon.

Move! Find Maggie before that cat does.

The inner voice spurred him to action. He signaled Lightning, quickening his pace. He'd been so angry when he found Colin's journal he could barely control himself. He'd been so furious in fact, it scared him to the point he'd contacted the VA for a counselor. He gone to group and private sessions, but instead of improving, his symptoms had escalated, so he'd avoided his wife all together. It was the only way to protect her from himself.

He called out Maggie's name, hoping he wasn't too late. He'd shut her out just as she'd accused, but he'd done it to protect her. He wouldn't fail her like he'd done with Colin.

∾

FIFTEEN MONTHS AGO...

Daniel grasped Colin's hand. "I've got you. I won't let you fall."

The ground shifted beneath him, throwing him off balance. Daniel gripped his hand tighter.

"Let me go."

"No!"

Colin's hand slipped from his and he vanished.

Daniel gasped in air, sweat drenching his body as he searched the darkness for Colin, until he realized the futility of his efforts. Colin was dead.

He'd saved hundreds of lives, why not his brother? He rallied at the injustice of it, as he had every day since Colin died. The hollowed out place in his chest where his heart used to reside pumped guilt and anger instead of blood, and consumed him day and night.

Daniel rolled to his side, and Maggie's soft breath warmed his face. He inhaled the subtle scent of peppermint toothpaste and strawberry shampoo. He longed to take her in his arms and silence the remorse that hounded him, but the tension between them had become a chasm that neither of them could cross.

Anger coiled through him as it did more and more frequently. It took little to set him off, and he could do little to control it. Right now his anger centered on Colin's journal that Maggie kept from him. What stung most was her loyalty went to Colin first—even in death.

Easing out of bed, he grabbed his clothes and went into the living room, needing to do something to relieve the tension inside of him. He made coffee, then dressed. When it finished brewing, he poured a cup, then stared out the window as the dawn drove away the darkness.

If only his grief could be relieved as easily as the coming of dawn. In the six months since Colin's death, he'd gone to the VA and attended group and private counseling, but his symptoms worsened. The only thing that offered some semblance of relief was work. He'd focused on making Adventure Docs the premier organization Colin had envisioned. And all long hours were paying off, but success carried a hefty price—sacrificing his marriage.

In truth, it was better that way since deep down he was terrified he'd take his anger out on Maggie.

The coffee soured in his stomach, and he poured it down the sink.

Lightning came up to him and whined. He rubbed his ears. "You ready to go skiing?"

His tail wagged.

They went out the back door, and Daniel slipped on his boots, then stepped into his skis. They took the trail that ran directly behind the house.

The early morning air chilled his face as he cut a path through the fresh snow. The silence soothed the anxiety churning inside of him until he passed the point where he'd found Maggie cradling Colin's lifeless body.

Daniel pushed harder up the steep slope battling the demons nipping at his heels.

Why hadn't he done something when he'd seen Colin's behavior spiraling out of control? He'd known his exploits were more than his usual daredevil stunts, yet he'd ignored Colin's obvious cries for help.

The sun crested the mountains, the bright light casting a golden glow over him. Instead of pausing to absorb the view, he headed back to the house, ate breakfast, then grabbed his keys anxious to avoid another scene with Maggie. All they seemed to do anymore was argue. Not true. They had plenty of uncomfortable silences, too.

He turned for the door and found her standing sleepy-eyed in the bedroom doorway staring at him.

The easy escape he'd hoped for vanished. "Sorry. I was trying not to wake you."

The softness in her face faded away. "You've become an expert at slipping away." Her calmly spoken words held the hint of accusation.

He didn't deny the truth of her remark.

She stepped closer. "Don't you have anything to say?" Anger and something more sizzled in her eyes—determination.

"What do you want from me?"

"I want some honest-to-god emotion from my husband. You do remember what that is, don't you?"

Yes, he knew, but talking to Maggie these days only generated more pent-up rage he wasn't sure he could manage. "I'm aware of what emotion is."

"Could have fooled me."

Daniel wanted to reach out to her, touch her, feel her velvety skin, but instead he curled his fingers into a fist.

Maggie stood toe-to-toe with him. "Why don't you just admit it?"

"Admit what?"

"That you don't want me anymore."

Not desire her? Never. This wasn't about her. It was about him—about his failure as a soldier, son, brother, husband. About the fury that he feared he'd turn on her.

Her accusation hung between them full of resentment.

The anger, never far away, simmered. "I need to get to work." He started for the door.

"I'm moving out."

The tenuous thread that had held them together these past months snapped. He froze, then slowly faced her.

"I won't be here when—if—you come home tonight." She released a bitter laugh. "This would be so much easier if you were cheating on me. Another woman is something I could fight, but indifference is a battle I can't win."

Her words were shrapnel to his heart. She'd finally given up. Not that he blamed her, but at the same time, she was abandoning him when he needed her most. Unreasonable, no question, since he was the one who'd pushed her away, but it was how he felt.

Daniel wanted to explain himself, but instead he remained silent. Until he managed his PTSD, he didn't want Maggie near him. He had to be certain he wouldn't hurt her. And if he told her, she'd only insist on staying by his side. It would be better to let her go.

So, instead of reaching out to her, he walked out the door, but what he really wanted was to take comfort from the woman he loved.

~

PRESENT DAY...

Since the first session at the VA, he'd tried two other private therapists, both specializing in PTSD, and the anger and nightmares still dogged him.

He'd made the right decision to let Maggie leave. Her safety was more important than his heart.

Maggie's words came back to him the first time she'd questioned why they were still together. *"This isn't a marriage. You don't confide in me or—" her voice had faltered, then her dark eyes glimmered with tears of hurt and defiance"—touch me. All we do is hurt each other. Why are we still married?"*

He'd had no answer for her then, and he still couldn't tell her the truth. He had to find a way to fix what was broken inside of him, because living apart from her was killing him.

The mountain lion yowled again.

Lightning's ears perked and his tail went high and stiff.

Daniel grabbed his collar, and he strained against his hold.

"Stay."

Lightning stared up at him with those dark, soulful eyes that wanted the same thing he did—to find Maggie.

17

Maggie faded in and out of consciousness. The fire flickered and died, the last of the wood was gone and she had no energy to search for more. All she wanted to do was sleep.

She watched the smoke trail into the dark sky, and Colin's shimmering image appeared through the haze.

There are no quitters in baseball.

The wind gusted and he vanished. She scoffed at his words. He would throw that back in her face. Okay, so maybe she wouldn't give up. She would get more wood, she'd keep the fire going.

She pushed to her feet and kicked the fire, urging more life from it to keep it going while she collected more wood.

The howl of a mountain lion cut through the perfect silence of the falling snow that was as terrifying as ending her marriage.

~

One year ago

When Maggie moved out, she thought being apart from Daniel couldn't hurt any worse than living with him.

Wrong.

Being apart didn't lessen the pain. Instead of just mourning for Colin, now she grieved for her breakup with Daniel, too. What she wanted was to crawl into bed and stay there. What she did was get dressed and go to work at Brother Murphy's.

Facing Liam and the barrage of questions about her breakup wasn't appealing, but if she didn't show up he or one of her other siblings or—she shuddered—her parents would come to check on her. As much as she loved her family, their smothering concern was not something she wanted to contend with right now.

Maggie drove over to Brother Murphy's determined to forget about her problems. She grabbed an apron from the kitchen, then pushed through the double doors into the u-shaped bar. The dark, lustrous mahogany glowed in the low light. Customers filled every seat, the mood lively and upbeat for a Wednesday night.

Noah poured a beer and pushed the mug down the bar. Jack O'Malley, a regular, snagged it with practiced ease, sipped, then continued his conversation with the curvy blonde sitting next to him.

Maggie scrounged under the counter for a pad and pen and tucked them into her apron pocket, then looked up at her brother. "So Liam roped you into working tonight, too."

Noah poured tequila into a shot glass. "I don't mind. It wasn't like I had anything better to do."

A pang of sympathy went through her. He and Sarah had called it quits on their twenty-year marriage, and she imagined he would have preferred to stay home and sulk. But he'd pulled himself up to face all kinds of well-meaning questions and sympathy. If Noah could manage, so could she.

"How are you doing?"

Maggie lifted a shoulder. "I've been better."

Noah finished pouring the shot and looked over at her. "I understand."

She was certain he did.

Liam's face appeared in the opening in the wall between the kitchen and bar. "Hey, get to work."

Maggie stuck her tongue out at him, then rolled her eyes at Noah. "He's a slave driver. It's no wonder he depends on us for employees."

Noah chuckled as she left the bar. The place was hopping with regulars and tourists, keeping her busy and her mind off her problems until she carried an order to the kitchen and found Daniel sitting at the bar.

She gave Noah her drink order, then forced a smile and faced Daniel. "Hi."

Why did her voice have to sound so damn breathless?

His dark eyes studied her in a way that sent tingles from the back of her neck to her toes.

"You slumming it tonight?" Daniel asked.

"I heard that," Liam called out from the kitchen. "For your information, working here is not *slumming it*."

"Your opinion," Maggie yelled back.

"Fact."

Their interaction drew a smile from Daniel, something she saw very seldom these days and she wanted to see more of, but it disappeared as quickly as it came.

"Well, I'd better get this order in to Liam."

She turned for the kitchen, but Daniel's fingers curled around her wrist before she could escape. It was the first time he'd touched her in months. She stared into his eyes. He looked haggard. Had their separation done that to him? Did he feel the same void inside that she did?

Before she stopped to think, she trailed her fingers over his cheek. He released her and recoiled as if she'd slapped him.

She stepped back, his rejection crystal clear.

"I'm sorry. I shouldn't have done that." He paused a moment, then continued. "Can we meet at the office tomorrow?"

"Why? What do we have to discuss that we can't do right here?" she demanded.

"There are some financial matters with Adventure Docs we need to go over."

Maggie blew out a shaky breath and resigned herself to meeting with him. "What time?"

"Whatever time works best for you. I'll be there all day."

She studied him closely, and it was like looking at a stranger. "Okay, I'll be by about eleven," she said at last.

"Maggie, orders up," Liam called, and for once she was grateful for her brother's intrusion.

"I'll see you tomorrow," she said, then made her escape.

When she returned from delivering her order, Daniel was gone and her dad leaned against the bar. She threw her arms around him and hugged him close. "Dad, I'm so glad to see you. Where's Mom?"

"Book club." He squeezed her tight, and the scent of sawdust and cedar drifted from him. "How's my champion?"

"Almost done with my shift. Will you join me for dinner?"

Her dad kept an arm around her shoulder and gave her a squeeze. "Would love to, but you realize it's after nine, so it's more a before bed snack for me. How about I have a beer while you eat?"

"Deal. I'll get my dinner while Noah pours your beer, then let's meet in the back."

Ten minutes later, they settled into a secluded table in the back. Her dad cupped the mug in his large hands. "So, what's got you down?"

Maggie lifted a shoulder, searching for an answer to his question. "Lots of things." She cut her chicken into bite-sized pieces. "I'm filing for divorce."

Her father's hand covered hers. "I'm sorry. I'd hoped you two could work out your differences."

She swallowed back the emotion that worked up her throat. "Me, too."

He was silent for a long moment. "Death changes a man. Some will open up and share, while other keep it inside."

Maggie sipped her wine. "I've seen plenty of suffering, too, but I talk about it."

Her father's eyes filled with sadness. "I'm aware of that, and as you know, I tried mightily to convince you to choose another career."

She remembered the pressure all too well. Not just from him, but her brothers and mother, too. "Why?"

He sipped his beer. "Everyone always says it's hard being a parent, and it is, but the hardest part is letting go. My instinct will always be to protect you, from the cruelties of the world, to a broken heart. You ignored my warnings on both, and I'm proud that you did. I was wrong, too. This is your life to live, and you've seen some terrible things, but you've made a difference. That's important. It makes for a worthy life.

"I was wrong about Daniel. I know you're hurting, but you two loved each other with abandon. That's a worthy love, and for all the heartache, you were good together."

Maggie ran her finger around the rim of her glass.

He touched her hand and she stilled the motion. "What else is eating at you?"

Maggie heaved a sigh. "I could never put anything past you, could I?"

He gave her a tender smile. "Nope, you were the one I could always read."

"Colin left me his share of Adventure Docs."

"I see."

Did he?

Instead of pressing her for answers, he waited for her to explain.

"I loved filling in at Adventure Docs before Colin died, and I'd planned to take over for him until Daniel and I started having problems." While she'd loved her job at Paradise General, she was sick of dealing with Dr. Rutherford's condescension.

"But," her dad prompted her when she didn't continue.

"I want to leave the hospital and work there fulltime."

Her father took another drink of his beer, watching her closely. "So, what's stopping you?"

She stabbed a piece of chicken, recalling her meeting with Daniel earlier. "It could be awkward working with Daniel."

He gave her that look he'd given her whenever she complained about not being as good as the boys. "It could be, but if this is what you really want to do, find a way to work with him. This is your life. Live it to the fullest, no matter what anyone says. Not me, not Daniel —anyone. You got that?"

She smiled, her heart lighter than it had been in a long time. She laid her head on his shoulder. "Thanks Dad. You always tell me what I need to hear."

He pressed a kiss to the top of her head. "I do my best."

And that was all anyone could do in this life was their best. She would tell Daniel her decision tomorrow, and he would have to accept it.

≈

MAGGIE ARRIVED at Adventure Docs at seven the next morning and found Daniel at his desk working at the computer.

"Good morning."

He tensed at the sound of her voice and faced her. "You're early."

She poured herself a cup of coffee. "I am. I wanted to talk with you before Sloan and MD arrived."

"What about?"

"I've made a decision that will impact both of us. I've given my notice at Paradise General. I'll be taking over for Colin at Adventure Docs fulltime."

His expression told her everything she needed to know. He didn't want her here, the idea of working with her day-in-and-day-out made him uncomfortable. She read it all in the flash before he schooled his expression.

With her dad's advice to live life to the fullest still fresh in her mind, she reminded herself this wasn't about Daniel and his needs, it was about hers. Colin left her his share of Adventure Docs because he knew she loved it, and that she would be a valuable asset. If Daniel couldn't see that, his loss.

As much as his rejection stung. She squared her shoulders and readied herself for a long drawn out argument. "I can see you're not pleased with my decision, but I hope we're both adult enough to find a way to work together."

Instead of commenting directly about her decision, he said, "I thought you loved your job at Paradise General?"

"I did, but I love Adventure Docs more."

A flash of anger, then infuriating calm closed down his features and sent a surge of anger through her. "Tell me what you're feeling. Stop shutting me out!"

His expression remained emotionless. "There's no reason to get upset. We will work out an arrangement."

The anger and frustration that had been building for months exploded. "I know that, but it's obvious you're not pleased to have me stepping in for Colin, so just say it!"

Her outburst hung in the silence that followed.

Daniel finally asked, "When do you plan on starting here?"

His calmly spoken words infuriated her to the point she blurted out, "Today, after I meet with my attorney to file divorce papers."

Another uncomfortable silence followed. Something flickered in his eyes that looked like disappointment, then vanished.

"I guess we'd better start by going over the financials," he said.

She watched as he turned back to his computer. What had happened to the man she'd married who displayed actual emotion?

That man was gone, and it was time she accepted this was all that was left of him.

~

PRESENT DAY...

Maggie hadn't wanted to file for divorce, but he'd left her no choice. She'd really hoped he'd ask her to reconsider, but he'd taken the news in stride as if she'd told him it was raining outside.

She might have lost Daniel, but she still had plenty to live for. A great job, family she adored, and plenty of friends. She grabbed the flashlight from her backpack.

Colin's image waved in the fading light from the fire.

You're a survivor Mags. Battle on.

Colin's voice gave her the push she needed to fight. If she could make it through the night, she might have a shot at surviving.

18

Daniel's voice was horse and his throat raw from shouting, but he continued calling out Maggie's name. He wasn't leaving this mountain until he and Lightning found her. He knew she was here, and he knew she was in trouble.

His phone buzzed, and Sloan's name came up on the screen.

"What have you got?"

"We found Maggie's car at Devil's Peak trailhead."

Confirmation she was here. She'd taken the east trail up—the more difficult route. That's why her car hadn't been at Pine Ridge where he and MD parked.

"Liam, Noah, and I are starting up this side while we can."

Daniel studied the snow falling. "What are the weather conditions over there?"

"We've got a light snow. How about you?"

"It's going from moderate to heavy."

"Shit."

"Ditto that. I'll keep going until I have to find shelter," Daniel said.

"Roger that. Stay safe."

"You do the same." Daniel ended the call, tucked the phone into the outside pocket of his backpack, then pulled his gloves on and started off again, his head lamp cutting a dim path through the snow.

He missed Maggie—touching her, holding her, making love, and the last time they'd been together had left him hollowed out inside.

~

Six months ago

Daniel drove down the narrow dirt driveway to Lake Serenity and parked in front of the cedar and brick house where Maggie was living. The deck went to the edge of the water. It was exactly the kind of home he'd hoped they'd find.

He got out of the truck and took the walkway to the door. He knocked and his mouth watered when Maggie opened it. The heavenly scent of marinara, garlic, and warm bread wafted outside.

"D-Daniel." Her voice caressed his name.

He couldn't tell if the catch he'd heard just now was pleasure or longing, but regardless, he liked the sound of it.

She let him in, and Lightning raced forward, tail wagging furiously. Daniel squatted down to pet him and received a slobbery kiss. He gave him a final pat, then followed Maggie to the kitchen, passing a table set for an *intimate* dinner for two—*not him*.

Resentment flared. He didn't want her having an *intimate* dinner with anyone but him.

"Would you like a beer?" she asked.

He shoved down the bitterness. "How about a dozen?"

"That bad?" She reached into the fridge for a bottle and opened it.

He took a long drink feeling it all the way to his toes. "No, just a long day." She limped over to stir the pasta, then replaced the lid and lowered the heat. "How's the leg?"

"It hurts like hell." She grabbed her glass of wine and hobbled into the living room where they could see the lake.

He and Lightning trailed after her. The view and the company soothed him.

He sat in the chair opposite her and Lightning laid his head on Daniel's knee. He rubbed his ears and asked, "What happened?"

"Lightning and I were doing some sprints and I pulled a groin muscle."

"Ouch."

"Yeah." Frustration pinched her features. "Probably going to miss the marathon I was training for."

"There will be others."

"You're just full of sympathy tonight, aren't you?"

Her sarcasm drew a grin. "You hate sympathy."

She heaved a sigh. "Almost as much as surprises. And this was one of the worst surprises."

He understood. He hated being out of the game, even temporarily.

"And I left us understaffed at the event today."

Daniel waved a hand in dismissal as he took another slug of his beer. "Could have been any one of us."

"So, I assume something happened or you wouldn't be here."

Her not so subtle attempt to remind him he avoided her, and he didn't deny it. He did it to protect her, but what he really wanted was to turn back the clock and share everything with her. Maybe then his insides would stop their continual churning, but instead he told her about the accident at the event.

"Two teenagers were seriously injured. One had a broken collar bone and ankle, the other a couple of fractured ribs, a punctured lung, and head trauma."

"Just because there were injuries doesn't mean we failed."

Daniel scrubbed a hand over his face. He knew that intellectually, but it still felt like a failure. "I know, but Colin—" His voice faltered for just a second, then he continued. "We always felt that as part of our service we should be able to offer prevention ideas to the event coordinators, so we always broke it down."

Maggie ran her finger along the edge of the wine glass, and he so wished that finger was touching him instead. "And since I've taken over for Colin you're here to hash it out with me."

"Yeah."

They watched the sunset, the glow of the sky reflecting across the water.

"Isn't this something we could have done at the office?"

It was, but he'd really come to check on her, to make sure her injury wasn't serious. At least that was the excuse he'd used. He'd really just wanted to see her. "It is. I should have called first."

"It's okay, and you don't need to call ahead. I don't mind you dropping by. Lightning misses you."

Lightning's tail thumped the floor as if in agreement.

He wanted to ask if she missed him as well, but didn't because he wasn't sure he wanted to hear her response. He had a hard enough time working with her every day.

She stared out at the lake a long time, then sighed. "How did we get to the point where we stopped confiding in each other? We used to do it effortlessly."

It was more of a comment than a question, but they both knew the answer. It was all on him. He'd shut down. He'd pushed her away and even if it was to protect her, he still longed for her. The urge to take her in his arms, feel the comfort of her warmth was strong—it's what he would have done before she moved out, but they weren't together any longer.

He pushed to his feet. "Thanks, but you're right. This is something we can hash over tomorrow. I mainly wanted to see how you were doing."

Maggie struggled to her feet, pain pinching her features.

Daniel cupped her elbow to help her up. He froze when their song came on the radio.

Their eyes met, and instinct took over. His arms came around her and they swayed to the music. He hadn't held her in months and he missed it—missed her.

He pressed his cheek to her hair and the subtle scent of crisp mountain air wafted from her the same as it always did.

Her soft sigh sent desire curling through him.

"Daniel."

The call of his name made him forget all the reasons he'd put distance between them. He wanted her, would always want her.

Her fingers trailed over his cheek. "Don't go."

Her whispered plea was his undoing.

He swept her into his arms and kissed her as if he was drawing his last breath, which he might very be because living without her had become unbearable. And she responded in kind, pressing her body tighter against him, then tugged on his T-shirt and back-stepped him to her bedroom.

They fell onto the bed and he stared into her face, imprinting this moment into his memory. "I love you," he whispered, the words coming deep from his core.

Her fingertips brushed over his cheeks as her eyes darkened. "I love you, too. I'll always love you." She pressed her lips to his. "Make love to me like there's no tomorrow."

∼

SMOKE WAFTED in from the kitchen followed by the screech of the fire alarm. Daniel yanked on his clothes, raced to the kitchen and shoved the burned pan of pasta in the sink, filling it with water, then opened the window to clear the smoke.

Maggie limped out just as he silenced the smoke alarm, tying her robe closed.

His eyes landed to the table intimately set for two and anger flared. Just like that, the intimacy between them vanished. "I should go."

She stared at him, a kaleidoscope of emotions reflected in the dark depths—regret, disappointment, loss.

She didn't protest his leaving, and deep down he'd secretly hoped she would—that she'd tell him their breakup was a horrible mistake, and she couldn't live without him, especially after what they'd just shared. Anger turned to fury, and the truth was, nothing had changed.

He wanted more than anything to drag her back to the bedroom and make love to her again, but it was better to leave her, than risk hurting her.

She followed him to the door, and when he stepped over the threshold, she softly uttered his name.

He faced her.

"I meant what I said. I will always love you, but loving each other isn't why we're apart, and you know that as well as I do."

Her words washed away the anger and left an emptiness that could only be filled by her. He wanted to reach out to her, the urge so strong he had to clench his hands into fists.

"I know, and I wish it could be different."

She stared at him a long moment, then whispered, "Me too." The door closed with a soft click, and he was alone on the porch.

The finality of her words resonated deep inside him. This time it was truly over.

∽

PRESENT DAY...

Daniel paused to adjust his pack, the darkness inside threatening to overcome him just as it had on Maggie's porch that night. Nothing had changed. The PTSD still had him in its grip. He'd looked into new treatments and tried a few, but still no relief and no hope.

Never give up.

Those words had been his motto through his military training and they gave him hope now, too. He would keep searching. He would find answers and get well, and he would find Maggie and bring her home.

19

Maggie started moving to warm herself and to remain alert. If she was going to survive the night she had to move. And while she walked, she worked on a plan. She knew this trail. There was a cabin less than a mile from here—the one she'd stayed in when she pulled her hamstring a few years ago. If she could make it there, she'd have an enclosed shelter and minimal supplies. It was her only chance.

She grabbed her pack, turned on her headlamp and cringed as pain shot up the back of her leg. She ignored it and kept going.

The headlamp cast an eerie glow through the snow, and she'd never felt more isolated or alone. She missed Lightning, wished he was by her side and prayed he'd survived the flood. If he were with her now, he'd find the cabin.

One step at a time, Mags.

Colin's encouragement made her smile, kept her moving forward. She lost track of the time, her entire focus on moving. She rounded a bend and saw the hazy outline of the cabin in the distance.

Relief shuddered through her along with another whole body shiver. She'd made it!

Within minutes she was inside the cabin, lit a fire in the woodstove, and began removing her wet clothes. Her hands shook so badly, her fingers barely worked. Finally, she slipped into the sleeping bag spread out on the bed. Her body shuddered violently as she attempted to get warm. Maybe it had been a waste of time to walk to the cabin. Maybe she'd die anyway—her last conscious thought before she drifted to sleep.

～

THE WIND INCREASED IN VOLUME, the snow so thick Lightning blended into the whirl of white. The cold penetrated Daniel's coat, and his fingers ached. If he didn't find Maggie soon, he'd have to find shelter and hunker down until morning, then resume his search.

Pale, yellow light momentarily flashed through the falling snow, then vanished.

Daniel quickened his step. The trail took a sharp corner and the light flickered again. He pushed on, praying it wasn't his imagination. The light grew stronger, his beacon to warmth and shelter.

The hazy image of a cabin came into view. He stumbled and pitched forward, his shoulder slamming hard against a rock as he hit the ground.

Lightning immediately came to his side.

Daniel's ears rang and his head swam. Pain ricocheted from his shoulder to his fingertips.

Lightning whined, but Daniel couldn't find the words to reassure him. Instead, he laid on the ground taking slow, deep breaths waiting for the pain to subside.

～

SOMETHING BANGED on the door disturbing Maggie's sleep. It sounded again, then the door swung inward, slamming against the wall. A blur of white rocketed across the room and leapt onto the sleeping bag. A warm, pink tongue lavished her with kisses.

"Lightning, you survived." Tears pricked her eyes.

He sat up and whined.

"What's wrong, boy?"

He jumped off the bed, stood in the doorway, and barked.

Wrapped in the sleeping bag, Maggie went over to close the door, but Lightning barked again and stepped onto the tiny porch.

"It's cold out there." She called him inside, but he ignored her command.

He grabbed her sleeping bag in his teeth and tugged her toward the porch.

She pulled free. "No come inside."

He barked again.

She kneeled down beside him and rubbed his neck. "What are you trying to tell me?"

Another bark, then a high-pitched whine.

Something was wrong. Maggie threw on her clothes. "Show me."

Lightning surged forward and she followed. A faint moan echoed above the wind.

"Who's out there?"

"Maggie?"

"Daniel?"

"Over here."

She followed the sound of his voice and found him on the ground. She dropped down beside him. "What happened?"

"I fell and hit my shoulder."

"Can you walk?"

"Yeah, as soon as the pain lets up."

"We can't wait out here in the cold." She carefully put her shoulder under his uninjured side, got him to his feet, biting back a gasp when pain shot up her leg. They fumbled their way to the cabin.

Daniel dropped his backpack and Maggie eased him onto a rickety chair. They both shivered violently.

Maggie put more wood on the fire.

"T-T-There's a sleeping bag in my pack."

Maggie fetched it and zipped it together with the one on the bed. She helped Daniel remove his clothes, then slipped off her own damp ones. They huddled together in the sleeping bag using their body heat to warm each other.

"Are you hurt?" Daniel asked, when the shivers eased.

"I pulled my hamstring—again, but other than that I just have some scrapes and bruises from when the flood swept me away."

"You were in the flood?"

"And Lightning." She reached over and stroked him. "I was so scared he didn't make it."

She saw Daniel's smile in the firelight. "He's the reason I found you."

Lightning whined and laid his head on Maggie's hip, staring up at her with adoring eyes that never missed anything.

"Thank you, boy."

His tail thumped and Maggie stroked him. "How's your shoulder?" she asked Daniel.

"Hurts like hell, but I don't think it's anything life-threatening."

"So you've said for the past five years. One of these days you're going to have to get it looked at."

Daniel's laughter filled the tiny room. "You've been harping about it for five years."

Maggie smiled, then yawned. Her last conscious thought before sleep overtook her was that their banter felt like old times.

She awoke much later—still in Daniel's arms. Her stomach rumbled.

"Same old Maggie. Always in need of nourishment."

She didn't deny his words, but she wanted a hell of a lot more than food. What she needed was nourishment in the form of him, but she didn't say that. Daniel handed her a nutrition bar from his backpack, then added wood to the stove, his naked body silhouetted in the firelight.

Maggie wanted desperately to touch him, and at the same time, seeing him this way made her uncomfortable and reminded her of all the times he'd turned away from her—even the last time they made love. He'd walked out when what she'd needed was for him to follow her back inside and never leave. The thought of another rejection stopped her from seeking physical comfort from him.

He took out his phone and tried to make a call. She heard the beep indicating no service.

She watched as he pulled on his clothes, wincing when he maneuvered his injured shoulder through the sleeve of his shirt. "Are we leaving?"

He looked at her, surprise on his face. "I thought you'd gone back to sleep. And no, we're not leaving. I need to contact MD and have him call off the search. I also need to let him know we'll be staying here tonight."

"I'm more than capable of hiking out." Had her tone sounded as desperate to him as it had to her?

He finished pulling on his boot, then stared at her with a searching look that she couldn't decipher. "I don't know about you, but I'd prefer to stay put until morning since we have to fight our way back down in the snow, especially with your hamstring and my shoulder, it will be much easier in daylight."

She couldn't deny the logic of his words, but she simultaneously dreaded and anticipated spending the night with him.

"Is the idea of being here with me that repellant?"

She was taken aback by his words. "No. Why would you think that?"

"The expression on your face."

She didn't know how to respond to that.

He tapped the end of her nose like he'd done so many times over the years and her heart thudded in her ears. She yearned for his touch, but instead he slipped on his coat.

"I'll be back in a moment."

Lightning raised his head, but made no effort to follow and curled back against Maggie. She gratefully absorbed his warmth and hoped Daniel hurried back—for his body heat and because she missed him.

Daniel came back inside several minutes later.

"Any luck?"

"Yeah, I reached him, and he's calling everyone back." Daniel stamped his feet to knock the snow from his boots, then undressed and slid back in beside her. He wrapped his arms around her and settled in, her back wedged against his chest. This was the closest they'd been in months, and she couldn't stop her body from responding, her mind from longing for more.

"Relax, Maggie. I'm exhausted and you must be, too. I'm not looking for anything, but to keep ourselves warm and sleep."

And that was the problem in a nutshell. She wanted him to desire her as much as she wanted him, but clearly he didn't.

His breathing evened out and eventually exhaustion overtook her as well and she slept, cradled in the arms of the man who would forever hold her heart.

~

DANIEL AWOKE with a start several hours later, the recurring nightmare of Colin's fall still vivid in his mind. His breathing came out in harsh, short gasps as he stared at the unfamiliar room.

Maggie rubbed his back as she'd done when they were together. Slowly, his breathing returned to normal and the tension left his body.

"Do you want to talk about it?" The soft murmur of her voice soothed him.

He tightened his hold on her. Inhaling, his senses filled with pine and a hint of strawberry shampoo. He remained silent, unable to share the nightmare and what he'd come to think of as his penance.

She squirmed closer, and the promise he'd made earlier became a distant memory.

Her audible sigh encouraged him as the nightmare faded away. He lifted her hair and kissed the side of her neck.

She arched back, allowing him better access.

His hand cupped her breast and she moaned his name.

She shifted so they were face to face, and her fingers brushed his face. Her direct gaze seared into his soul. "I want you, Daniel. Make love to me."

It was all the encouragement he needed. With only the firelight to guide them, they found each other again.

~

THE NEXT TIME Daniel awoke soft light filtered through the cabin window and every detail of their lovemaking, every touch, every sigh, came back to him. But with daylight, came the realities that separated them.

He slipped out of the sleeping bag and dressed. He didn't trust himself with her, and that reality throbbed more painfully than his erection.

He added wood to the fire, then searched the tiny kitchen and found a pot. He placed it on the woodstove and added water. While he waited for it to heat, he searched his backpack for coffee and MREs.

"Please tell me you have coffee and food in that endless backpack of yours."

The croon of Maggie's groggy voice sent desire straight to his groin. "I never leave home without it."

"Always the Boy Scout, aren't you?"

His eyes locked with hers, and he wanted nothing more than to climb back into that sleeping bag and prove he wasn't a Boy Scout any longer with another round of lovemaking. But he didn't. Instead, he focused on preparing their coffee, then handed her a cup.

Their fingers brushed and Maggie's body immediately responded the same as it had during the night. She wanted him again with an intensity that couldn't be denied.

Maggie blew on the scalding coffee, savoring the heat that soaked into her fingers. She sipped it and it warmed her, but even with the fire, the room was icy.

She reached for her clothes, the bruises and cuts from the day before making their presence known. The walk down would not be pleasant.

"You don't have to get up. It will be a while before the rescue team makes it up to us."

Maggie gave him a hard stare. "Rescue team? That had better be for you because I'm more than capable of walking out of here on my own."

Daniel shot her a skeptical look. "I'm fine, but between that pulled hamstring, all those bruises and scrapes you may want to rethink hiking down."

"I'll be fine once I get moving."

His scrutiny made her self-conscious. He'd seen her naked hundreds of times, but the things they'd done earlier left her feeling vulnerable and uncomfortable to bare herself in front of him. Sex was one thing, intimacy another.

Apparently, he sensed her discomfort because he turned away while she dressed.

She managed to get her clothes on with only a few grunts and groans.

"Still ready to hike down the mountain?"

She sat on the sleeping bag and pulled on her socks. "I've felt worse. I'll manage." In fact, she'd experienced a lot worse. Some of the triathlons had left her sore, aching, and blistered for days.

"Daniel, I'm not trying to be stubborn or difficult—but after last night it just feels," she paused trying to find the right word, "awkward between us."

His dark eyes filled with understanding. "I'm sorry about what happened. It won't happen again, I promise."

Her heart stilled.

He moved away from her. Maggie took in the tense set of his shoulders and the stubborn expression on his face. "I never said I didn't want you to touch me."

"We're divorced."

The finality of his tone hurt more than his silence or the angry words they'd hurled at her other since Colin died. It was over. She needed to accept that and quit hoping for miracles.

The stubborn set of his jaw made her equally obstinate side dig in. "It's always the same between us, isn't it?" she said. They went around and around like a hamsters running on a wheel, always circling back to the same thing. He kept pushing her away and there was nothing she could do if he wouldn't meet her halfway.

Finally, Daniel said, "Nothing has changed."

The tone of his voice hinted at something more than resignation.

"What is it you're keeping from me? I'm a big girl, Daniel. Whatever it is I can take it."

For a moment, she thought he'd tell her, but then his eyes took on that faraway look she'd seen too many times since Colin died.

The sex might still be amazing between them, but without intimacy, what did they really have? She wanted all or nothing. She'd hoped they could find a way back to each other, but it was time she accepted defeat. This was one battle she wasn't going to win. And the realization left her empty inside.

20

They met up with MD and the rest of the search party midway down the trail. Maggie walked back even though they'd brought a stretcher.

"I'm fine and I'm walking. Would anyone care to press me?" Her gaze circled the small group and no one said anything, not even MD who usually had a wisecrack. "Okay, then let's get moving."

She brushed past Daniel.

When they got down to the cars, she had MD drive her and Lightning to her car over Daniel's insistence she go to the hospital.

She gave him a cool stare. "If anyone needs medical assistance, you do. Get that shoulder looked at."

Daniel ignored her comment. "I still think you should go to the ER."

He could think what he wanted. She was going home. She whistled to Lightning and put him in the back of MD's truck, then climbed inside.

MD drove her to the trailhead and parked, then faced her.

"I'm really glad you're okay."

"Thanks, me, too." She paused, her throat working as she tried to formulate her next words. "I'm going to sell my share of Adventure Docs back to Daniel."

He was silent a long minute. "What will you do?"

"I'm not sure. I just know I can't—" She stopped short of telling him she couldn't be around Daniel any longer. "I need a change."

"I'm going to miss you."

"Ditto that. Let's you, me, and Sloan have a beer before I leave."

"Yes." He hesitated. "I'm sorry it didn't work out."

Tears stung her eyes, but she kept them at bay. "Me, too. It's not how I envisioned this ending."

"Me, either. I just wish—"

She shook her head. "Let it go. It's over."

MD nodded, hugged her, then she and Lightning climbed out of his truck.

Maggie waved, unlocked her SUV, and put Lightning in the back, then drove home. Rather than mope, she called her brother and arranged a family dinner at the pub for that evening. She had her family to lean on, and she would bask in their love and affection. But would it be enough?

$\approx$

A WEEK LATER, Maggie ended the call. She should have been ecstatic that she had her old job back, and that Dr. Rutherford had retired, but she couldn't summon so much as a Hooah. All she saw were lonely, empty days stacked out in front of her. At least she could lose herself in her work.

She put on her snow shoes and walked over to see Abby and her nephew. Her life was back on track, except for the empty black pit that replaced her heart. That would never be filled.

She knocked on the door and heard the thundering of tiny feet as they raced to the door. A cherubic face pressed against the long window next to the door.

"Aunt Maggie!"

Jon jumped up and down and clapped his hands, then tried to turn the doorknob, but he couldn't open it. "Mama, Aunt Maggie is here," he screeched. "I can see her in the window."

"I heard you, Jon. Everyone on the lake heard you."

Maggie saw the laughter in Abby's eyes as she pulled open the door and Jon barreled through. He wrapped his arms around her legs.

Maggie bent down, scooped him into her arms, and swung him around.

His delighted squeal was music to her ears. She squeezed him tight. "I've missed you."

He pushed back far enough to put a big, sloppy kiss on her cheek, then squirmed to be put down. She set him on his feet, and he ran off to the living room.

"Tea?" Abby asked.

"Please."

"I thought you'd be at Adventure Docs today."

"I'm not working there anymore. I got my old job back at Paradise General."

Abby faced her as they entered the kitchen. "Why? I thought you loved working at Adventure Docs."

Maggie sat at the bar. "I do but, I'm done—finished. It's time I faced reality. Daniel and I are never going to be together. It's over between us and working with him is just too painful."

Abby put the teapot on and opened her mouth to respond when Jon came racing into the kitchen. "Mama."

She squatted down on his level and pressed a kiss to his forehead.

Maggie envied her brother and sister-in-law. They had the life Maggie had envisioned with Daniel. She'd wanted children and a forever-after with Daniel, but all she'd gotten was heartache.

"Drink, Mama."

Abby handed him his sippy cup. He took a long drink, then handed it back.

"What does Daniel think of your decision?"

"I don't know. I haven't spoken with him yet." Maggie stared out the kitchen window to the turbulent water on the lake, reminded yet again of her loss, of the fact Daniel wasn't by her side any longer.

Abby leaned against the counter. "You do know he cares about you."

"I know he does, but his love for me was never the problem." Maggie heaved a shaky breath. "We're either a couple that's there for each other or we aren't a couple. I want a marriage like my parents have. It's not perfect, but they talk to each other, they listen, they support one another. I won't settle for anything less."

The teapot whistled. Abby lifted it off the burner and filled their cups, then came around and sat down beside Maggie, squeezing her hands.

"Don't settle for anything less. You deserve it all."

Maggie blinked back tears. "Thank you."

∾

Daniel leaned back in his office chair and stared at his cell phone the same as he had for the past week. Ever since Maggie told him she was selling her part of Adventure Docs, he'd wanted to call her and beg her to reconsider. He'd also wanted to call and find out how she was doing. He'd had progress reports from everyone, but that wasn't enough. As much as he wanted her back, he couldn't risk it.

He closed the office and drove over to Brother Murphy's, went inside, and sat down at the last open table in the back corner.

The waitress came by and he ordered a beer. She left him a menu while she got his drink.

Liam brought the beer and sat down across from him. "Hey, about time you dropped by to see me."

"Sorry. Been busy."

"Too busy to come by and see your friends?"

Daniel sipped his beer to stall while he came up with an answer that would satisfy Liam and take the conversation in another direction. "Been trying to get caught up at work."

"Twenty-four/seven?"

"It works out that way sometimes when you have your own business, especially now that Maggie sold her half of the business to me."

"Okay, true. But take it from me, don't let the job run your life." He got to his feet. "Maybe you should consider taking on a couple of partners."

Not a horrible idea. "Who?"

"Boy, sometimes I see why you and Maggie are such a perfect fit. You can both be pretty dense sometimes. I'd bet Sloan and MD would be interested."

Daniel let that sink in a moment and slowly nodded as he realized it was a great idea. "Thanks, I'll think about it."

"Speaking of a job that rules your life, I've got to get back to the bar. Do you want dinner?"

"Yeah. Give me a burger and fries."

"Done."

Ethan Burke came in. He taught eighth grade with Maggie's brother, Noah. "Hey, Liam."

"Hey, Ethan. What are you doing out on your own?"

"Clare and Ben are checking out a college back east and visiting her parents this week so I'm on my own."

Liam stepped back. "Well, Daniel's on his own, too. You two should share a table since we're packed tonight."

"Do you mind?" Ethan asked.

"Not at all," Daniel lied. He was lousy company these days, but he didn't say that. Ethan would discover that soon enough.

"What are you having?" Liam asked.

"One of those," he gestured to Daniel's beer, "and a burger and fries."

"Coming right up." Liam headed back to the bar.

Ethan settled into the seat across from Daniel. "So you asked me to keep you posted if I heard of any property coming up for sale on the lake."

Two years ago he'd have jumped on this opportunity, but now he had no reason to. Without Maggie, it was pointless, but curiosity got the better of him. "Where is it?"

"It's about a half mile south of where Jon and Abby built their place."

Just what he'd wanted once upon a time, but now it had lost its appeal.

"If you're interested, you'll want to look into this soon. I know for a fact there are other buyers who are looking at the property."

It would be an opportunity to build his own house from the ground up—something he'd always wanted. But he'd wanted that with Maggie. Then again, maybe it would be something to keep himself busy and forget about the one hundred and one ways he'd fucked up his life. "Do you know who to contact?"

"I do. It's an older gentleman who just lost his wife, and he's decided he doesn't want the property any more. I'll text you his name and number."

A moment later his phone dinged.

"Thanks."

"So, how's your dad doing? I haven't seen him in a while."

Daniel tried to decide how to answer that question. His dad had taken Colin's death hard. But he was doing much better now, far better than Daniel. He was engaged and moving on with his life, while Daniel was mired in anger, self-loathing, and isolation.

Finally, he said, "It's been hard."

Ethan took a sip of his beer. "I sure get that. Clare and I still struggle some days, and it's been almost four years now since we lost Grace. Thank God I've got her to lean on or I would never have made it."

"It's hard, especially when—" Daniel stopped just before saying he should have saved Colin.

Ethan studied him over the rim of his mug. "Especially when you feel responsible for his death." He took a sip, his gaze never wavering from Daniel's.

He supposed if anyone understood what he was feeling it was Ethan. His daughter had died in a boating accident, and he'd been unable to save her.

"It's not uncommon to feel this way, Daniel, but it doesn't mean you are responsible."

Daniel snorted and took a long drink of his beer. "Doesn't mean I'm not, either."

Ethan set his mug down. "Tell me you didn't do everything within your power to save him."

Daniel didn't respond, his mind flashing back to those last moments with Colin. He'd tried to convince him to hang on. He'd nearly fallen trying to rescue his brother. He'd saved so many, why not Colin?

Their food arrived and Ethan said nothing until the waitress left. "Let me tell you something I've told few people other than my counselor and Clare. I blamed myself for Grace's death. I should have known the weather could change, I should have left sooner, I should have driven the boat in a different direction, I should have rescued her even after I was knocked unconscious."

"You couldn't possibly have known or done any of that," Daniel said.

Ethan pointed a French fry at him. "Exactly, but I didn't believe it until my counselor pounded it into my head, and on a bad day I still have those thoughts. What's important is I don't let them destroy my life, or Clare and the boys. I was definitely headed in that direction. I was about to lose them, but that counselor saved me, brought me closer to my wife and kids and my parents than I'd ever been."

Ethan pushed a business card across the table.

Bruce Whitman, therapist.

Daniel stared at it before tucking it into his pocket. He'd already tried counseling, but maybe it was worth one last try. Anything to end the anger and flashbacks that just kept getting worse.

"One more thing and then I'll quit preaching. You have to find someone that works for you, so if Bruce isn't the guy, keep looking."

True to his word, Ethan changed the subject and started telling him about his classroom of rambunctious eighth graders that he clearly loved, but the whole time Daniel's mind kept circling back to the name and number in his pocket. What if Ethan was right? What if he just hadn't found the right counselor? But what if no one could fix what was wrong with him?

~

MAGGIE DRAGGED herself out of bed, made coffee, and stood at the window staring out at the few remaining patches of snow trying to decide what course to take with her career the same as she had for the last month since she'd gone back to work at Paradise General.

She loved working at the hospital, but she'd loved Adventure Docs more. She wished she could have stayed there, but it just wasn't possible.

She and Daniel walked on eggshells around each other, and she couldn't imagine continuing to work there—especially when a lasting relationship with Daniel wasn't in the cards.

She wanted a husband and family, something Daniel couldn't offer her, so it was time to start over—maybe somewhere new. The idea of leaving family and friends left her heart heavy, but a fresh beginning held a lot of appeal.

She was already moving so that Abby and Noah and Jon could move in here. They needed more space with the new baby coming. They'd offered her Noah's house, but they intended to sell it and she didn't see the point in moving, then having to move again when they sold it—unless she decided to buy their house, but she wasn't sure that was something she really wanted.

She went to shower and then head to Adventure Docs. She'd promised to do one last job. She loved the team, the work—she even loved the team leader. But that was the problem in a nutshell. She couldn't keep working there when every time she saw Daniel it was a reminder of what could never be.

~

AN HOUR LATER, Maggie pulled into Adventure Docs to go over the ski race they were covering at Serenity Mountain this weekend.

Sloan and MD were already inside tossing a football. She intercepted a pass as she walked to her desk.

"Maggie *Invincible* Gregorio intercepts Mad Dog and rushes it to the end zone." Sloan used his best sportscaster voice, his coffee mug acting as a microphone.

"The crowd goes wild." Sloan held the mug out to MD.

MD began cheering and waving.

"You two are a crackup."

"Hold on and we'll have a special interview with *Invincible* after the game."

Their antics drew a laugh from her.

Sloan came over and leaned a hip on her desk as she put her purse away. "What are you doing here?"

"Last I checked I still worked here unless you guys replaced me."

Sloan drew back in mock horror. "Replace you? Never!" He looked over at MD for confirmation.

"No way we could get along without you," he agreed.

While they were teasing, behind the banter was sincerity. She would miss these two. Working with them had always been fun, but beneath their antics, they were good at their jobs—in fact, there was no one better.

She winked at them. "I'm sure you'd find someone stronger and more capable."

"But never *Invincible*," Sloan said.

"That's right, Mags, you're one of a kind."

She smiled, forcing back the tears gathering in her eyes and did what they expected from her—gave back as good as she got.

"You two blow more blarney than me sainted old grandmother," she said using her best Irish brogue.

They hooted with laughter and went back to their desks.

"Where's Daniel?" she asked.

Sloan shrugged. "He said he had an appointment and would be in later."

"No specific time?"

"Nope, sorry."

Daniel called that afternoon only to say he had personal business to take care of and left the planning of the ski race to the three of them. Most likely he was avoiding her, which left her relieved and disappointed.

21

D aniel stared out the second-story window to the churning waters of Lake Pend Oreille mimicking the emotion roiling through him.

"Daniel." The therapist's voice pinged through his brain. "Have the flashbacks lessened since our last session?"

"Yes." He hadn't had a nightmare in over a week, but still it took very little to trigger his anger.

Bruce glanced at his notes. "Let's talk about Colin today."

The absolute last thing Daniel wanted to do. "What about him?"

"Were you close?"

"Yes. We were friends and business partners."

"What about your personalities?"

"Similar, but Colin was far more reckless than I was."

"In what way?"

A smile inched up Daniel's lips. "From the time we were small, he accepted any challenge. One time, my friend Liam and I built a ramp to jump our bikes over two garbage cans. We cleared them no problem, but Colin insisted he could make it over three, and he did."

His smile faded and his hands curled into fists. Tension threaded between his shoulder blades and crawled up his neck. "I remember another time the school called to tell Dad that Colin had climbed up the stadium lights at the football field. Dad asked what the damage was, and they said nothing. He was just sitting up there. They wanted Dad to keep him down. Dad told them he'd try, but he made no promises."

"Do you blame your father for not doing more to curb Colin's behavior?"

No, he blamed himself. He'd promised Mom he'd take care of him and he'd failed. "We all had a hand in it."

"Because you think discouraging his behavior would have made a difference?"

"Yes."

"Have you and your dad discussed this?"

The anger blazed hotter and he answered through gritted teeth. "Yes."

"And what was his reaction?"

"He said stopping Colin would have been as impossible as trying to hold back the wind, and doing so would have destroyed his spirit."

"So he supported your brother, but you didn't agree with him."

"I didn't."

"Were you right?"

Daniel ran a hand through his hair, his voice barely a whisper of sound when he spoke. "Yes."

"Tell me about the accident."

He didn't need this. His hands clenched tighter and tension coiled in his gut. He didn't want to relive it, but Bruce had told him from the start of their sessions talking gave him control of his emotions.

Still, he considered walking out the door, and he was ready to do just that until it hit him that's exactly what Colin would have done. And look how he'd ended up.

He'd come here for help, and no matter how painful, he was sticking it out.

"We went mountain biking. The trail was rough and covered with debris, but Colin flew down it anyway." Daniel closed his eyes remembering it all as clearly as if it happened yesterday. "Colin's bike hit a tree and sent him flying over a ledge. I grabbed him. The branch snapped. I had him. I wasn't going to let him fall, but he let go."

The sudden silence made him uncomfortable.

Bruce's gaze bore into him. "Is it possible your brother let go to save you?"

It had occurred to him, and the idea that Colin had sacrificed himself infuriated him.

"Why does that make you angry?"

Daniel pounded his fist against the window frame. "Because I should have saved him. I should have held on tighter, leaned out further—I promised Mom I'd take care of him." Daniel's voice broke and the anger metamorphosed to fury. He wanted to smash the window, punish himself.

"What about your wife? Do you blame her for not doing more?"

He didn't want to discuss Maggie. "She did the best she could."

"Couldn't you say the same about yourself—that you did everything in your power to save Colin?"

He flexed his fingers. "It wasn't enough. If you knew about—"

"About what?"

Bruce was a damn heat-seeking missile he couldn't shake. He stayed on his tail and kept coming.

"On Colin's last tour in Afghanistan, his team was sent to flush out a group of terrorists hiding in a village. A mother and child came toward them, and Colin was ordered to take them out, but he couldn't do it. The mother ignited the bombs strapped to her and the boy. Colin's best friend was killed, and he blamed himself." The knot in his gut twisted tighter.

"Stop bottling up your anger. Hit the punching bag." Bruce gestured at the bag hanging from the ceiling.

Daniel had resisted using the punching bag his first session, but the past two sessions he'd pummeled it and it helped. He pulled on the gloves and pounded the bag. Sweat drenched him and he kept punching, drowning out the voices, the negative buzzing in his brain. He wheezed in air, but kept punching until he couldn't lift his arms.

"Better?"

Daniel swiped the perspiration from his forehead with his arm. "Yes."

"The key is to release the anger in productive ways, don't keep it pent up inside." Bruce held out a bottle of water.

Daniel took it from him and guzzled it down, then moved back to the window and studied a flock of geese flying low over the water, wishing he'd known. Wishing he could have eased his brother's pain.

"Did Colin tell you what happened?" Bruce asked.

Daniel shook his head. "I found his journal after died." White, hot burn-down-the-house anger surged again. The journal Maggie had hidden from him.

"Colin told Maggie about the journal when he was dying and asked her to destroy it, but she didn't."

"Why does that make you angry?"

He wasn't angry, he was livid at the idea that Colin had confided in Maggie and not him.

"Daniel, this doesn't work if you don't talk to me."

Bruce sounded just like Maggie.

"Colin and Maggie were always close. They had a connection that went to another dimension. With just a look, they knew what the other was thinking."

"You were envious of their bond?"

"Hell yes!" Confessing it aloud eased the tightness in his chest. "Maggie and I didn't connect like that. Don't get me wrong, we were good—really good together." Daniel pressed a hand to the window, the cold seeping into his palm and penetrating into his heart.

Bruce pressed him. "So you wished you'd had a deeper connection with your wife?"

"Yes."

"Why do you think you held yourself back?"

"I had to."

"Why?"

Daniel's jaw locked and the tension inside him grew. "Because I was afraid to open up to her—to anyone."

"Why?"

He shot Bruce a lethal glare. "You just have to keep pushing and poking the wound, don't you?"

Bruce's calm demeanor infuriated him even more. "What is making you so angry?"

"I don't know." He shouted. "I'm always angry—so angry I was afraid I'd hurt her, so I pulled back." Admitting it out loud, the rage left him in a rush and he sank down onto the sofa weak-kneed.

"What did she do that hurt you so deeply."

Daniel swore, then pushed on as if he were going into battle. "She left me." Pain seized his chest. Rather than ignore it, he acknowledged it, and spewed out his fury, pain, and abandonment. "She promised to stand by my side, but she left me when I needed her most."

~

DANIEL LEFT Bruce's office with a list of anger management techniques for PTSD sufferers. The other counselors had given him similar brochures and he'd thrown them all away. But whatever was happening with Bruce, he was making progress and four weeks later, he'd seen the benefits of the techniques. He scanned the list. Some of them looked silly, but he'd finally reached the point he didn't care. He'd try them all if that's what it took to get well.

He stared at number five. Talk about the anger—with family, friends, other veterans. That would be the hardest, admitting to his family and friends he had a problem.

He started the truck and headed back to Paradise Falls. Ethan had been right. Counseling wasn't for sissies. Having his fingers severed one by one would have been less painful. Instead of going to the office, he went home, changed into his ski clothes, and hit the trail out his back door following the second suggestion on the list—exercise. He set a grueling pace and followed the trail until he reached the lookout that opened into a view of Paradise Valley. To the left Lake Serenity, and Maggie's house, to the right, the snow-covered Rockies.

He'd heard through Liam that Maggie was applying for jobs in Spokane and even contemplating another stint with WHC.

She could easily get a job at either place with her experience. All those years they'd traveled the world, he'd supported her, but now he didn't want her to leave. He wanted her to stay here—with him.

He wanted a different ending to their love story. He just didn't know if he could make it happen, but he was determined to give it a shot. His biggest hurdle—convince Maggie he deserved a second chance.

～

DANIEL STARED at the contract to buy Maggie's half of the business the same as he'd done for the past six weeks. He didn't want to sign it. He wanted her to stay on at Adventure Docs, but that wasn't reality. She'd returned to the hospital, and last he'd heard, she hadn't decided if she would stay on permanently.

Daniel wanted to tell her about the changes he'd made to his life, but he was afraid she'd tell him it was too little, too late, and he couldn't blame her after the way he'd behaved.

"Did you hear Maggie had a job offer in Spokane?" Sloan asked, intruding into his thoughts.

Daniel scowled at him. How the hell would he have heard that, and then realized from the smirk on Sloan's face that he'd been taunting him. He glanced at MD and his father who was working part-time as their mechanic, both clearly interested in his response.

Sloan threw another taunt at him. "You know she didn't want to leave here. She loved working here."

"I didn't fire her. She sold me her half of the business."

"Only because it broke her heart to work side-by-side with you." Sloan kicked his feet up on his desk and leaned back in his chair. "So when are you going to man-up and go after her?"

Silence.

Daniel's gaze traveled from Sloan to MD to his father. They all waited for his response. "She left me."

"Because you were being an ass," MD said, taking obvious pleasure in needling him.

Daniel threw up his hands. "I'm still an ass. Why would she take me back?"

"Because you're an ass who's learned how to be less of an ass, how to talk about his problems instead of holding them inside until they explode," his father said quietly. "The counseling is working. We've all seen it, and I for one admire you for seeking help."

Sloan and MD nodded in agreement.

His father continued. "Don't keep putting off going after her or you will regret it. There are lots of women in the world, but few who are as perfect a fit for you as Maggie."

They'd all told him to do what he'd wanted to do for the longest time, but the fact was, he was a coward. Fear kept him from going to her. They were right. If he kept stalling, he would definitely lose her. He took his keys and wallet from his desk drawer and headed for the door.

"Where are you going?" MD called after him.

"Where do you think?"

"Do you need backup?" Sloan rose from his desk.

"Hell no! You three have done enough prodding. The rest is up to me."

He walked out the door to more jeers and taunts, but ignored them. He was a man on a mission, and he wouldn't stop until Maggie booted his ass off her property or he won back her heart.

⌇

DANIEL DROVE straight to Maggie's to find her car loaded with boxes. He parked behind her and sucked in a breath, building the courage to face her.

Just your heart in the balance, Gregorio. No big deal.

He got out and knocked on the door.

No answer.

The lights were on inside and he could hear Lightning barking. She had to be here somewhere.

He walked around to the deck and saw a lone figure staring out at the ice-covered lake.

He followed the path and stopped when he reached her. She turned, her eyes bleak and empty. He missed how they used to light with pleasure the instant she saw him. He'd sucked the happiness from her, and he would regret that for the rest of his life.

"Daniel. What are you doing here?"

Good question. To beg for forgiveness.

"I need to talk to you."

"If it's about Adventure Docs, I've made my decision."

"It's not. It's about us."

She stared at him, her expression blank. "There is no us."

His fault. "I know, and I've given you no reason to listen to me, but I wish you would."

An otter did a belly flop on the ice and slid across the frozen water. Any other time, its antics would have brought a smile to Daniel's lips, but not today.

"Five minutes," she said.

Five minutes to pour his heart out to her wouldn't be nearly long enough to win her over, but he had to try.

"Okay, first I'm sorry about my reaction to the journal. The truth is, it was the excuse I'd been looking for to put distance between us, but I was also jealous of your relationship with Colin. You two connected on a level that transcended words, and that's something I've always wanted between us—with Colin, too. I just never felt as close to either of you as I thought I should, but that distance had more to do with my PTSD."

Maggie's expression remained neutral. She started to speak, but he held up a hand stopping her. "Please let me finish."

She gave him a single nod.

"I've been going to counseling for the past six weeks and it's helping—a lot."

He watched the otter a moment as he gathered the courage to continue.

"I'm glad you've found someone to talk to, and I appreciate you telling me this, but I really need to finish packing."

He shifted his gaze to her. "I still have three minutes."

"There's more?"

"Yes." Now for the difficult part. "I'm sorry I wasn't there for you when Colin died. My PTSD got worse after his death—the flashbacks, the anger. They scared me. When they started I could control the anger, but it just kept getting worse. I've seen too many vets snap and hurt their loved ones and I was afraid I was going to do that, too, so I pushed you away. I've learned that's the worst thing I could have done. It's not an excuse. It's just what happened. I've been carrying around a butt-load of guilt. I-I should have saved Colin. I should have done more to get him help." Regret tormented him yet again. He sucked in a ragged breath." I should have held on to him."

"Why didn't you tell me this before?"

"I thought I was handling it and I was afraid—"

"That I'd blame you?" Her chest puffed up with righteous indignation. "I would never do that—never."

Clearly. "I'm sorry—sorry for everything. For not confiding in you, for thinking that you would judge me."

"Why are you telling me all of this?" she asked.

He'd known she'd ask that, and he still didn't have an answer for her, so he spoke from the heart. "Because I've come to realize that I never really opened up to you. I always held a little of myself back. I wanted us to be close like you and Colin were, but I never really put myself out there." He paused, then pushed on. "I want to try again. Give me another chance, to show you I've changed—that I can be the man you need."

Maggie's heart thumped. She'd longed to hear these words for so long. She'd tried so hard to make their marriage work even though she'd seen no response from him. And now, when she'd finally moved on with her life, he wanted to try again.

"Why now?"

Tension coiled in the air between them. "When you went missing, I died inside. I didn't want to go on living without you, and I realized that you are the one person I can share anything with. But I'd pushed you away, kept everything I was going through to myself when all I really wanted was your comfort and support."

Did she dare open herself up to him again? Did she have the strength to endure more heartbreak if it didn't work? She shuddered at the thought of more lonely nights crying herself to sleep, but could she walk away from the man she still loved more than her next breath when he came to her heart-in-hand?

Self-preservation kicked in, reminding her she didn't have a choice. There was only so much rejection she could bear before she started dying inside.

She took a step back. Being so close, inhaling his scent, staring into those eyes that had sent joy, anticipation, and lust through her tempted her to give in.

She took a sharp inhale. "I'm sorry. I can't do it again. I love you, Daniel. I'll always love you, but I can't go through this again."

His shoulders slumped and the utter despondency in his eyes left her raw and emotionally spent.

"I understand. You've moved on."

Moved on? A bitter laugh built in her chest, but she restrained it. She turned and walked back to the house before she changed her mind.

Just when she thought she'd escaped, he caught up with her.

"Maggie."

She halted her flight, but didn't turn around because she didn't want him to see her vulnerability or the tears pooling in her eyes.

"You dropped this."

He held out the letter she'd been reading just before he arrived.

"I'm sorry, I read it. I shouldn't have, but I couldn't stop myself."

Her hand shook as she reached for it.

"It looks like a good offer, but I hope you're not leaving Paradise Falls because of me. If you are, don't leave your life and your family. I've hurt you enough. I'll move Adventure Docs."

She took the paper and squeezed it tight in her fist. Unable to formulate a response, she looked up, the tears she'd held at bay streamed down her cheeks as she watched him walk to his car.

Colin's voice echoed in her head.

Don't be a fool and let him go.

"Daniel." Her voice came out a whisper of sound that faded away with the wind.

She raised her voice. "Daniel."

He stopped, but kept his back to her, his body tense. Slowly he pivoted to face her.

He's always held your heart and soul.

A truth she couldn't deny.

"I turned down their offer. The truth is, I can't leave Paradise Falls again. I'm here to stay. I want—need stability in my life."

"I'm glad. Your family will be happy."

"What about you?"

He swallowed, the muscles working in his throat showing his emotion more clearly than words. "I'll do my best to stay out of your way."

She shook her head. "That's not what I meant."

His brows drew together. "What do you mean?"

"I mean, are you happy that I'm staying, too?"

Anticipation replaced confusion. "Spit it out, Maggie. What are you saying?"

"I'm saying I want to know if you were serious when you said you wanted to try again."

His eyes glistened with unrestrained pleasure. "Really?"

She nodded and another flood of tears streamed down her cheeks. "Yes."

He ran to her, scooped her into his arms, and swung her around. Maggie tilted her head to the sky, snowflakes drifting onto her face.

He set her on her feet, and his hand trembled as his fingers brushed her cheek. "I swear that this time I won't let you down."

Maggie smiled. "This time we'll both do better."

He held out his hand. "Deal."

"This needs to be sealed with a kiss."

He swept her into his arms and kissed her, sweet and chaste, then hard and demanding. Her pulse thumped in her ears and she wanted a whole lot more than a kiss.

"Take me to bed or lose me forever," she quipped against his lips, using the line from an old movie.

The heat of his gaze set a fire burning deep within her. "Show me the way home, honey."

And she did just that—she took him inside and he left his mark on her forever and always.

EPILOGUE

Maggie pulled on her warmest gear to ski up to the shelter at Eagle Point to watch the Northern Lights with Daniel. They'd been back together for almost a year, and while they'd had their challenges, every day got better and better.

Instead of going dark on her when he had a bad day, he told her what he was going through. It wasn't perfect. It was messy, just like life, but she could live with that.

Noah, Abby, and Jon had moved into Abby's lake house, and she and Daniel had rented Noah's home from him until they made a decision about their future. They'd bought the land Ethan had told them about, but so far it remained vacant. Maggie was ready, more than ready to make a decision, but she didn't know where Daniel stood.

He hadn't pushed her and she'd appreciated that, but now she wondered what held him back.

Daniel walked in and leaned over her shoulder to nuzzle the exposed skin on her neck. "You know we could stay home, cuddle, and watch the lights from the bedroom window."

Maggie stepped back. "Oh no. I'm not missing this. We can come home and cuddle later."

He released a put-upon sigh. "Okay. Are you ready?"

"Yes."

They reached the shelter an hour later and Daniel built them a fire. When he stepped back, she slipped her hand into his. "Have I told you lately how much I love you?"

"Yes, you have, but I can't hear it often enough."

She smiled and pressed a kiss to his lips waiting to hear the words from him. When he said nothing, she said, "Well?"

"Well, what?"

"Do you love me, too?"

"Do I really need to say the words?"

She bounced on the balls of her feet. "Yes!"

"Maggie Gregorio, I will love you with my dying breath." He dropped to his knee and took out a velvet covered box. "Will you marry me—again?"

The ring she'd returned to him sparkled in the firelight. "Oh, Daniel."

Her hand trembled as she ran a fingertip over the diamond.

"I need an answer."

"There's something you should know first."

"What?"

"I'm pregnant."

His whoop echoed down the valley. "That's the best news ever. And you know what that means, don't you?"

"No, what?"

"It means we don't have time for another fancy wedding, which is what you

wanted the first time."

She brushed her fingers across his cheek. "You know me so well."

He kissed her fingers and Maggie sighed. Life wasn't perfect, but it was damn good.

The end

～

If you enjoyed *The Murphy Clan* in *Falling in Love for the First Time*, here's a sneak peek of *Forever His*, from the *Return to Hope's Crossing* series and part of *The Murphy Clan series.*

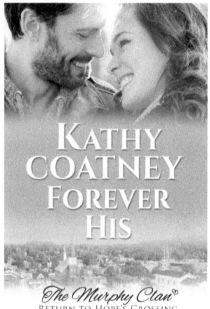

Hope's Crossing, Indiana

Sam Parker navigated his dark blue SUV through the slice of road narrowly cut between the endless acres of mid-July-high corn.

"Are we there yet?" His eight-year-old son, Kevin, repeated the age-old question for the third time in the space of thirty minutes.

"Almost."

"That's what you said last time."

Sam understood his impatience, but he felt the opposite. Instead of being relieved they'd reached their destination, tension pulsed between Sam's shoulder blades. Would coming home be enough to end the rift between him and his father?

Unlikely. Joe Parker had never understood why Sam had chosen a professional baseball career over farming. And he was certain that in the nine years he'd been away, the old man hadn't mellowed. When his father took a stand, he held it to the bitter end.

The familiar pristine-white church steeple rose above the towering stalks, acting as a beacon over the emerald sea of cornstalks.

Sam eased off the gas when he approached the corner of Glory Lane and Main Street, and he caught a glimpse of the white picket fence that circled the cemetery. Memories thick as cobwebs crowded him. He hesitated a moment, his heart thudding in his chest, then continued into town.

The corn suddenly parted and gave way to a line of square brick buildings. Silver maple trees in full summer uniform tossed shade over his SUV as he cruised down Main Street. Would he receive a hero's welcome from the town? Doubtful.

Kevin's blond head bobbed as he bounced on the passenger seat. "Will I see my grandpa soon?"

The bitter taste of regret lodged in Sam's belly like one too many donuts for breakfast. He forced a smile. "Yes."

"How far is it to the farm?"

"A couple of miles."

This was the most animated Sam had seen the boy since he'd come to live with him six months before. Rarely did he get more than a yes or no response, and it was generally followed with silence.

Surprisingly, Kevin had been downright exuberant when Sam told him they were going to Hope's Crossing to see a grandfather he hadn't known existed until two days ago.

Sam hadn't had the heart to tell him the real reason for the trip— that his grandfather had leukemia, needed a bone marrow transplant, and that without it, he would most certainly die.

Kevin had enough on his shoulders after his mother's abandonment six months ago, and then her death days later. Sam wanted to spare him another loss, but he would have to tell Kevin the truth, and soon.

The marquee of Mumford's Theater towered above the downtown buildings. The Friday night hotspot for throwing Jujubes and watching G-rated movies with his brother, Ryan, his best friend, Griffin, and *Emma*.

Sam braked suddenly when he spotted Emma's ancient, battered Ford truck parked underneath the garish neon-red sign that flashed *Beauty Bowl: Food, Bowling and All-Around Family Fun*. Luella Lorraine Lavell's pride and joy—a bowling alley, local eatery, beauty parlor and community center all rolled into one.

He pulled in next to Emma's truck and memories of sultry summer nights, bare skin glowing in the moonlight, and soft laughter dancing on the summer breeze filled him.

"Why are we stopping?"

He shook off the past. "I thought we'd grab some lunch before we went to the farm."

"I'm not hungry. I want to see the farm." Kevin folded his arms over his chest and turned to stare out the window, the animated child replaced with the sullen little boy.

Sam swore under his breath. Every time he made headway with Kevin, he did something to screw it up. Of course, he could hardly blame the kid for his reaction. They both knew Sam was stalling, and facing Emma was preferable to confronting his father. But explaining the rocky relationship he had with his father was beyond his abilities and an eight-year-old's comprehension.

Sam ruffled Kevin's hair and he jerked back.

Stung by his son's rejection, Sam retracted his hand. "We will, but first I want to introduce you to some old friends of mine."

Sam pushed open his door and stepped out into the sticky midsummer air. His knee gave slightly when he put his full weight on it. The collision at home plate a year ago during the playoffs had not only ended his professional baseball career, but left him with several surgeries and months of physical therapy. The doctor had assured him that his knee would heal eventually. It would never be strong enough to play baseball again, but he should have general use of it. Still, it had been a year, and he was coming to the conclusion this was as good as it got.

He took another step, and when the knee held, he walked to the passenger side and opened the door. Kevin obediently got out and followed Sam into the Beauty Bowl without a word of complaint. His compliancy troubled Sam. Keeping his emotions bottled up inside wasn't healthy, but every time he'd tried to get Kevin to open up he'd been met with a wall of silence.

The cow bell clanked when Sam opened the double glass doors.

Some things never changed.

The gray-haired McDonald sisters still sat at the front table facing the street. All the years Sam had lived in Hope's Crossing, they'd sat in that very spot watching the residents of Hope's Crossing stroll past while they sipped coffee and gossiped about the local citizenry.

Sam flashed them a smile and nodded. In response, they gaped at him. He quickly guided Kevin across the black and white checkerboard floor, ignoring their whispers. Instead, he focused on the woman with the strawberry-blonde ponytail seated at the revolving chrome and vinyl fountain stool.

His gaze swept over Emma, down the slope of the soft, smooth skin visible at her neck, to the trim waist, to the narrow booted feet hooked over the chrome rung of the stool.

Stopping behind her he leaned forward and caught a whiff of that unique blend of purple prairie clover and sunshine that he always associated with her. He watched her dip a spoon into her signature treat.

He leaned closer to whisper into her ear. "Still got a thing for fudge sundaes, I see."

A sharp intake of breath followed his comment, then she squared her shoulders and slowly swiveled on her stool. His breath stalled when she faced him fully. She was still a cool drink of water on a blistering summer day.

He studied the average nose and evenly spaced eyes. Most wouldn't discern a single standout feature, but Sam knew better. When she smiled the ordinary became the extraordinary, setting fire to her eyes and turning the dull green to bewitching velvet.

That smile had been his light once, and her gentle laughter the sustenance for his heart and soul—until his brother, Ryan, found them together. After that everything that had been good in his life went to hell, except for baseball. He'd clung to his career like the life-saver it was. And now that was gone, too.

"You came." Her eyes locked with his. Eyes that spoke emotion without words. Eyes that spoke of the pain of death, and regret—and disappointment in him.

It took a moment for her words to penetrate into his brain, and when they did, he bristled. "Did you honestly think I'd have ignored your call?"

Her chin inched up a notch, the green of her eyes deepening. "I honestly didn't know. It's not like you and Joe have been on the best of terms since you left here."

"I left you a message. Didn't you get it?"

"That was two days ago."

"I got my affairs in order and came. Has something changed? Is he worse?"

A flicker of fear crossed her eyes, then resignation. "No, nothing has changed."

His anger melted away as rapidly as the ice cream in her dish. He had no right to be upset with Emma. Any blame fell squarely on his shoulders. He was the one who'd allowed nearly a decade to pass and made no effort to breach the abyss between him and his father.

And why?

Pride. It had kept him from driving home and ending their feud. And now his father was seriously ill, possibly dying, and did he call his only surviving son to tell him? No, he'd left that duty to Emma.

The only reason he was here now was Emma. If it had been up to his father, he might not have found out until it was too late.

An ear-piercing screech echoed over the smack of a bowling ball knocking over a set of pins.

"Sam Parker, as I live and breathe." Luella launched her bowling pin shaped body out from behind the counter and into Sam's arms, rocking him backward. "It's about time you came home."

"Luella, you're looking as beautiful as ever."

"You sweet-talking devil, you. This town hasn't been the same without you." She gave him a squeeze that he swore cracked a rib.

Resisting the urge to rub his side, he drew Kevin closer. "Kevin, I want you to meet Emma Delaney and her aunt, Luella Lavell. Ladies, my son, Kevin."

Kevin stared up at Luella's mass of brilliant straight-from-the-box pomegranate red hair with the ever-present Smokies baseball cap perched on top.

It was difficult, if not impossible, to read the name of the team with all the baseball pins attached. How Luella held her head up beneath the weight of them, Sam couldn't fathom.

"Fine lookin' boy. Looks to me as if he could follow in his daddy's footsteps. You play baseball?" she asked Kevin.

"Yeah."

Luella gave him an approving nod. "Baseball is the only sport there is—next to bowling that is. Do you like to bowl?"

Kevin hunched his shoulders. "I dunno. I've never done it."

Luella arched a dark penciled brow above red, cat-eye rhinestone glasses. "Did you hear that?" she demanded to the room at large.

From the corner of his eye Sam saw Emma purse her lips to restrain the smile that threatened. Bowling was serious business, and Luella believed it was God's game, and the cure-all for anything that ailed a body, not to mention she was a faithful believer in the three B's—bowling, baseball and the Bible.

Pressing a hand to her heart, Luella exclaimed, "Blasphemy." She perched one hand on her hip and shook a finger at Sam with the other. "What kind of parent deprives his child of the spiritual experience of bowling? Have you no shame? Have you forgotten everything I taught you? You never would have been the baseball player you were without bowling."

Sam did his best to hide his amusement and present an appropriately contrite expression. "I waited until I could bring him to the best —you. I didn't want just anyone teaching my son about something as important as bowling."

Luella sniffed, then nodded, her outrage appeased. "I knew I'd taught you well." She studied Sam, then Kevin. "Well, what do you two want to do first—eat or bowl?"

Sam rubbed his stomach. "Eat."

"Bowl."

A smile tilted Luella's hotsee-totsee red lips. She clasped her hands together. "Praise the Lord. I've got another believer in my midst."

Luella glanced over to Sittin' Pretty, the beauty parlor that her niece, and Emma's cousin, Cassie Cooper, operated. "Jeff, come over here. There's someone I want you to meet."

Sam grinned as a boy about Kevin's age wiped grimy palms on his white T-shirt, leaving parallel smudges of dirt down the front.

"Jeff and his older brothers, Tyler and Trevor, are staying with Cassie until their dad comes back." Luella turned to Kevin. "How about Jeff and I teach you the finer points of bowling while your father fills his belly?"

Kevin immediately brightened. "Really?"

Luella gave a firm nod of her head. "That okay with you?" She posed it as a question, but Sam's agreement was clearly an unimportant afterthought.

And really, what did he know about raising a kid? He'd taken Kevin in without a thought about the realities of raising a child alone. He struggled with the basic day-to-day details of getting him fed and clothed, but Kevin had plenty of psychological issues that left Sam completely bewildered. And what kid wouldn't have emotional problems after being abandoned by his mother, then have her die in a plane crash? So yes, he'd turn over care of Kevin for a few minutes to someone with experience and knowledge about the workings of children.

Sam nodded at Luella. "Yeah, it's fine."

"Good. Jeff, help Kevin find a bowling ball." She turned to Sam. "What do you want to eat?"

"Cheeseburger, fries and a soda."

Luella nodded. "I'll have it ready in a jiffy. Have a seat, and you can catch up with Emma while I fix it." The devilish gleam behind those rhinestone glasses told Sam she was hoping for a whole lot more than reminiscing between them.

Knowing Luella, she'd be working overtime to get him and Emma back together. That would never happen. He'd walked out on Emma when she'd needed him and that was unforgivable. He'd blown his chance with her, besides which, Emma loved farming as if it were her own personal slice of paradise, while he placed farming right up there with having a root canal without Novocain.

Order Forever His!

Need more of a good thing? Get *The Murphy Clan's* Return to Hope's Crossing series.
Download now!

ALSO BY KATHY COATNEY

Thank you for reading *Falling in Love for the First Time,* part of *The Murphy Clan. The Murphy Clan* can all be read as stand alone books, but there are also three series within the Clan—*Falling in Love, Return to Hope's Crossing, Crooked Halo Christmas Chronicles,* and a *Vermont Christmas Romance.* If you enjoyed the characters of Paradise Falls, be sure and check out the Falling in Love series and the entire Murphy Clan.

If you liked this book, I'd love it if you'd leave a review at Goodreads and BookBub.

I love hearing from my fans. You can contact me through my website, newsletter, or join my Facebook group Kathy Coatney's The Beauty Bowl. I share information about my books, excerpts, and other fun information. If you like free books come join Kathy Coatney's Review Team by sending me an email kathy@kathycoatney.com.

All my books are small town, contemporary romances with uplifting stories of hope, a sprinkling of quirky characters and a happily ever after.

Contact me at:

Website

Kathy Coatney's The Beauty Bowl

The Murphy Clan

Falling in Love series

Falling For You…Again

Falling in Love With You

Falling in Love For The First Time

Falling in Love With Him

Return to Hope's Crossing series

Forever His

Forever Mine

Forever Yours

Crooked Halo Christmas Chronicles

Be My Santa Tonight

Her Christmas Wish

Under the Mistletoe

A Vermont Christmas Romance

Santa Comes to Snowside

Box Set

Falling in Love Box Set

Crooked Halo Christmas Chronicles Box Set

ABOUT THE AUTHOR

I've spent long hours behind the lens of a camera, wading through cow manure, rice paddies and orchards over my thirty-year career as a photojournalist specializing in agriculture.

I also love—and write—deeply emotional, small-town contemporary romance. Ironically, some of my books carry an agriculture thread in them, some more than others. Please note I used to write these books under Kate Curran, but now I write all books under Kathy Coatney.

I also writes a series of nonfiction children's books, From the Farm to the Table and Dad's Girls.

When I'm not writing, you'll find me mountain biking, cross-country skiing, or running—a really, really slow jog that's been compared to a pace slower than a tortoise.

f 𝕏 **◎** **BB** **g** **𝓟** **a**

CPSIA information can be obtained
at www.ICGtesting.com
Printed in the USA
LVHW041327080722
723038LV00005B/529